Alexander Merow

Prey World

Alexander Merow

Prey World

Hatred and Faith

Novel

Part III

Bibliografische Information der Deutschen Nationalbibliothek:
Die Deutsche Nationalbibliothek verzeichnet diese Publikation in der Deutschen Nationalbibliografie; detaillierte bibliografische Daten sind im Internet über http://dnb.dnb.de abrufbar.

Translation: Alexander Merow

Verlag: BoD • Books on Demand GmbH, In de Tarpen 42, 22848 Norderstedt
Druck: Libri Plureos GmbH, Friedensallee 273, 22763 Hamburg

ISBN: 978-3-7583-5057-3

Chapters

'What is the greatest talent of the tick? It is the ability to fall on a dog and crawl through its coat to find a place to suck blood - without being noticed. This is the great skill nature has given to the tick.

But even thousands of ticks can not rule over a dog's life. To the contrary, they can only suck their host dry and kill it in the end, because nature didn't also give the tick the skill to reign. And it is the same with our enemies. In the moment, when they take over this world, their rule will start to crumble...'

Artur Tschistokjow in 'The Way of the Rus', chapter VI 'The Enemy Unmasked'

'We must use the methods of the World Enemy to fight him. I know that it is a terrible truth, but we have no other choice if we want to survive. This is a fight to the death for us, for our nation and also for the rest of mankind. Everyone, who follows me, must be aware of this.'

Artur Tschistokjow in 'The Way of the Rus', chapter VIII 'The Iron Rules of our Movement'

Artur Tschistokjow

It was raining outside and darkness had fallen over the bleak estate of prefabricated houses in the southern part of Vitebsk. Artur Tschistokjow was sitting in his kitchen and thoughtfully played with a little shot glass which was dancing between his fingers.

He took another sip of cheap swill and stared at the wall with his bright, blue eyes. Today, he was more nervous than ever before because the GSA, the international secret service, was upon his heels. Agents of the World Government had come to Belarus and were intensively searching for him. This was no pleasant situation. But here, in this gray ghetto of apartment blocks full of poverty and dreariness, they would not find him.

Artur was not registered anymore, he had no more Scanchip and he left his apartment, which had been rented by an unremarkable person, only in case of necessity. His friends supplied him with food and paid his bills.

There was no other way. Artur was always quiet and appeared to his neighbors as a shadow, when he walked down the corridor of his floor in the night, never saying a word. He had no more telephone and no Internet connection. This was much too dangerous in a time of total surveillance.

Artur Tschistokjow had vanished in order to live a ghostly life. No official data base could find him anymore - and this was his only chance to survive. Artur went to the fridge, an ugly, battered thing in the corner of the room, and took out a sandwich. Then he sat down in the living room and opened the next bottle of vodka. This life was painful, but it was still better than being caught and liquidated. The young man stroked through his stringy, blond hair and his long face with the pointed chin became a tragic mask. He looked out of the window, but there was nobody. Only the rain, the darkness and an old street lamp with a loose connection which was flashing all the time.

Some of the windows in the opposite block of flats were still illuminated. Who lived his life behind those curtains? Perhaps a man who was just as unhappy as Artur After a few hours, he fell asleep on the couch. This day was over.

In the early morning hours of the next day, Peter Ulljewski, Artur's best friend, brought some bread and a dozen sausages. Peter was 34 years old and a craftsman. A few months ago, he had moved to Vitebsk, together with Artur, and was now living in a small apartment in the outskirts. When Artur heard the latest news, he became even more nervous.

'They have arrested two of our men last night. Andrej and Igor', Peter said. 'Both were distributing our leaflets when the cops caught them.'

'Two men less...,' muttered Artur, falling back on the sofa.

'But this looks good, right?' remarked Peter, pulling a thin newspaper out of his pocket. He gave it to his friend. Tschistokjow examined everything and finally nodded.

'Yes, it's a great work, Peter. My editorial about the new administration tax is on the cover page. Nice!'

'We will print about 10000 copies of this edition. I told our young comrades that they have to be more careful, when they distribute our promo material,' returned Peter and took a bottle of soda out of the fridge.

'At first, we will spread our newspapers and leaflets only in Vitebsk - and only in estates of prefabricated houses. In quarters like this we will get the most encouragement from the population', remarked Artur with a serious face.

'What's about the stickers?'

'About 20000 are in print,' replied Ulljewski.

'Okay! Better than nothing.'

Artur tried to smile again, then he went to the window. 'And the group in Minsk?'

'They want 20000 stickers too', said Peter.

'If there is some money left, then we print them as fast as possible,' explained Artur; he drew the curtains.

'Three days ago, you have been on television. They have shown a picture of you and asked the people for information,' told Ulljewski.

'I already know that - from Vladimir,' returned Artur quietly. 'Was something in the papers too?'

'Just a small article about our spraying last Tuesday. Nothing important, but meanwhile they know us. And they seem to pay a bit more attention to our actions.'

'Certainly!' murmured Tschistokjow pensively.

'Anyhow, everything is ready for Saturday. What's about your speech, Artur?' asked Ulljewski.

'I work on it! Don't worry. I know enough things to say. This is our smallest problem, my friend.'

Some minutes later, Peter said goodbye and left the room silently.

'I'll pick you up at 18.00 pm,' he finally said and shut the door behind him.

Artur looked nervously around, while he thought about all the possible incidents that could happen during the meeting on Saturday. He prayed that everything would run smoothly, because even a little gathering was dangerous enough for him. If the police or the GSA would ever catch him, it would all have been in vain. Two years ago, the young man from Kiev had taken over the leadership of the 'Freedom Movement of the Rus', a patriotic, anti-governmental organization of Belarusians who wanted to liberate their homeland from the tyranny of the World Government.

At that time, Artur had still lived in Minsk. Meanwhile, the once tiny faction had become a small political factor because of its restless and effective publicity campaigns. Many people seemed to have sympathies for the 'Rus', but now the authorities and even the GSA followed their traces and they would not rest, until Artur was in their hands. The enemy knew that he was the leader of the organization, and the hunt for him had already started.

Even television had reported about him several times, in the usual way. He had been called a 'terrorist' and a 'dangerous lunatic'. Furthermore, they had put a bounty on his head, although he had so far just published political pamphlets and had never been violent. If Artur had to leave his apartment by day, he had to creep out like a rabbit who was searched by a pack of gun dogs.

Artur did not catch his neighbor's eyes so far. Otherwise, the police would have already visited him. He shunned the inner city of Vitebsk which was meanwhile cluttered with cameras and eye-ball-scanners. His older brother and his parents had been arrested a year ago. With this tactic they wanted to lure him out of his hiding place but he was still nowhere to be seen. The probability was high that his family members had already been liquidated, because he had heard nothing from them since months. But to look for his parents or his brother would have been suicide.

Because of all this, Artur's hatred had grown enormously. Nevertheless he still felt helpless. Although an increasing number of Belarusians had barely Globes to live and were more discontent than ever before, only a small group of men had joined his organization. Most people were too scared of losing even the rest of their pathetic existence.

The authorities threatened to block the Scanchips of all who supported or joined the 'Freedom Movement of the Rus' in secret. In the worst case, helping the Rus could mean imprisonment or execution. The situation was terrible for everyone involved, and slowly the concerns of the once so creative and fun-loving young man were eating him up from inside.

'I cut off, if necessary, to Japan. If I can't stand this hell anymore,' said Artur sometimes to himself and felt a little more relieved then.

But this feeling never lasted long because the fear in his head was always there.

'Goal!' screamed Frank Kohlhaas enthusiastically and turned around to his teammates.

His best friend and today's opponent, Alfred Bäumer, looked angrily at him and clenched his teeth. Frank had once more humiliated him with his soccer skills.

The goalkeeper shot the ball across the field and the match went on.

'Give me that thing!' heard Frank his teammate Sven shout from the other end of the field.

Kohlhaas jumped up; header, goal. Alfred landed in the dirt again and cursed.

'Bäumer, even my grandma is faster!' laughed a young man of Frank's team. Alf growled at him and angrily kicked the ball out of the way.

The game still lasted for a further hour. Today, it was sunny and warm. An ideal day for a football tournament in the Lithuanian village of Ivas.

Finally, Frank's team could defeat the other three teams from the tiny village and he walked off the field with a satisfied grin.

'What was wrong with you today, dude?' asked Frank the frustrated Alf with sardonic undertone.

'No idea! Maybe I just wasn't fit. Next time, we will sweep you from the field!' grudged Alf and uttered a silent snarl.

Julia Wilden gave Frank an admiring glance and the young man answered with a broad smile.

'Franky, go!' she shouted and made a victory sign.

'I dedicate my last goal to you, fair maiden!' called Frank and gave Alf a nudge in the ribs.

'Fuck off!' whispered Bäumer. He sat down on a stool.

It was a wonderful day. Julia was giving Frank all her attention and literally idolized him. Her father, the head of the village community, clapped on his back and praised him too.

'I didn't know that you are such a great dribbler.'

Frank was happy. Today, he had thought not a second about the horrors of the Japanese war which had haunted him so many times in the last months.

The politics, the war and everything else seemed to have vanished in the distance. And Frank was glad about that.

'Let's go to Sven for a drink!' suggested Alf and made the impression that he had calmed down.

'Good idea, old man,' said Frank with a short laughter.

They went back to the village and finally visited Sven who was waiting for them with a beer case. The two friends hadn't had so much fun since months.

It was Saturday and the meeting was planned for today. The old warehouse, somewhere in the countryside of northern Belarus, was filled with nearly 200 people who were eagerly waiting for Artur Tschistokjow's speech.

Except for a few abandoned farm houses and large fields, there was nothing around them. The leader of the 'Freedom Movement of the Rus' looked nervously out of the window beside him. Meanwhile, it was 19.00 pm and it was slowly getting dark.

'I hope there are no informers among the people,' said Artur quietly to himself, breathing heavily, full of worry.

The fear that the police would suddenly approach, tortured him since hours. Some of his men stood near the entrance with guns in their hands, willing to defend themselves if the cops would try to arrest them.

The leader of the group of Minsk, Mikhail, opened the gathering and got a thunderous applause. He railed against the Belarusian politicians who served the World Government as administrators of the country. He called them 'traitors', 'criminals' and 'bloodsuckers'.

The discontent men, who had come to the meeting, wanted to hear things like that. It sounded like music in their ears, in a time when all hope seemed to be lost. A

13

comrade from Gomel turned around to Artur and asked him to begin with his speech. Tschistokjow walked up some stairs and went to a speaker's desk which his fellows had made for him.

The front part of the desk was covered with the flag of the organization. Artur's heart started to pound faster, while his comrades applauded. A young boy came to the stage and said reverently, 'I'm proud to meet you personally, Mr. Tschistokjow. I have seen a report about you on television.'

The leader of the Rus smiled at him and beheld the naive appearing group of men in front of him. They looked up to him like believers to a priest. But what could he really give them?

'Not even a mouse has to fear us,' he said to himself. Then he spoke to his followers.

'My dear comrades! I welcome you to this meeting of the 'Freedom Movement of the Rus', our organization, which is fighting the ruling system with all its limited resources.

There are some new men and women here today, some unknown faces. This is the way it should be. I hope that the coming hours will be peaceful, and that no policemen will disturb us. Today, we are about 200 people in this dilapidated building. It is no great number but it is better than nothing.

You all risk your heads, when you come to us and join the fight against the occupation regime. I admire your courage, my comrades. And we will need brave men and women in the coming struggle for freedom. But what else remains for us in these days? Shall we better continue to keep quiet? Shall we just try to survive by crawling from one bad paid job to the next? Trying to become not one of the homeless people, by keeping our mouths shut in front of our masters?

No, this can not be the right way! We must defend ourselves and we will defend ourselves! Last week, the lackeys of the World Government in Minsk have started a new raid against our people. Raising the tax for administration, increasing the prices for electricity. Even lower wages for those, who still have some kind of work, and so on!

They leave us no more air to breathe. They draw the noose tighter and tighter, squeezing the life out of our people. We should remember the better times. Times when a farmer could live from his yield, and a worker from what he had earned. Times when we had something like an own culture and were free men and women. Now, we are slaves, and our country goes, slowly but surely, down the drain. Meanwhile, the Belarusians have just a few children because it has become to expensive to raise a family.

Today, our young people have to emigrate to other countries to find work. Anyone, who loses his job and doesn't find a new one in time, ends as a beggar, becomes homeless - and finally just dies.

In return, the World Government brings hundreds of thousands of foreigners from Asia or Africa to our country in order to get rid of the old Belarusian population. If you walk through some parts of Minsk, Moghilev, Grodno or Gomel, you no longer believe that you are still on Belarusian territory. They want to create a patchwork of different nations, races and cultures on our soil, because this patchwork won't resist them anymore.

We, the Belarusians, shall die out and disappear, if you listen to the speeches of Medschenko and his bunch of traitors.

The media pollute our minds with lies and meaningless entertainment every day. They want to brainwash our nation and distract us from our misery. But a small group of people here in Belarus is not poor, not at all! I'm talking about the group of collaborators in Minsk, the group of betrayers. They have a good life by squeezing out their own people! Sub-governor Medschenko is such a tick, and his whole staff of helpers too!'

'Hang this son of a bitch!' shouted one of the men through the hall.

'Medschenko and the rest of the traitor scum must be killed! Put them up against the wall!' screamed a young man, raising his fist.

The other people yelled and applauded. These words were like balm for their frustrated souls. Artur Tschistokjow continued and slowly all the fear was falling from him. He seemed to become a giant who spoke with passion and inner fire.

'We demand that this country shall be independent again! Free from the global system of enslavement! We demand, that this country shall be governed only by Belarusians who serve their own nation! This land belongs to the Belarusians, not to the occupiers, the World Government or other foreigners!' he shouted and his supporters cheered.

Artur banged his fist on the desk and gave his men a determined look, his narrow face was quivering with excitement.

'But we should not fool ourselves. Those, who oppress us, will continue to serve the exploiters and won't become reasonable or sensible tomorrow! They won't use the few Globes, they can still squeeze out of us, to build new schools, kindergartens or to generate more jobs. No! They will only give us more cameras, more paid informers, and will even call more GCF soldiers to our land so that we can feed the oppressors with our money! Furthermore, our country is totally indebted by the 'Global Bank Trust', but there seems to be still enough money to finance all the surveillance!

We must still dwell in the dirt while they tell us that the coffers of Belarus are empty, but this is a lie! They have money but not for the people of Belarus. However, for GCF soldiers, for monitoring and for the foreigners who live on social welfare!'

'Right!' yelled an old man, clapping his hands.

Others also applauded and nodded at Artur. He continued.

'When I decided, some years ago, to resist the destruction and looting of our fatherland, it was clear that I would soon reach a point of no return. Back then, I swore, I would make this country free again and give it back to its rightful owners - the people of Belarus.

I'm often scared that they find and kill me one day, but we all shall not fear our enemies because we are the fighters for the future of our children!

Our movement will not rest until this country is finally free, and our countrymen shall no longer fear hunger and misery! If we die trying, then it shall be! What do we have to lose? I prefer standing in front of you, just for an hour,

17

as a free man, than living a hundred years as a supervised, soulless slave!

And from now on, there will be only one rule of us all: Spread the word! Carry our fight to all parts of Belarus! We have to go to the agency workers in the remaining production centers of our country! We have to go to the countless, homeless people, who have already lost all hope! We have to go to the families, to tell them about the political goals of our movement!

The people of Belarus are becoming more and more desperate and we need to show them that there are other options than just being enslaved!

We must bring the good news to the masses, tell them about the coming liberation. Our brothers and sisters out there are waiting for a change, they are waiting for us, my comrades!'

Artur's speech still lasted for two hours. He spoke about global politics, the Japanese war of independence, the economy of Belarus - shouting his postulations through the meanwhile half-dark hall.

Finally, he presented some of his own concepts. Artur talked about how he wanted to make Belarus free and independent again, how to give the masses work and how revive the old Russian culture. In the end, he was only content with some parts of his speech, but his followers answered him with loud cheers and adored him.

Finally, his supporters gathered around him, trying to talk about everything again. They praised him and for a moment Artur felt euphoric. Shortly afterwards, he discussed the next steps with his group leaders. One of them proudly told him that he has even won a high-ranking official of the civil service as a sympathizer. The event, which had taken place far away from any nosy eyes in a little village near Vitebsk, ended calmly and all the guests went back home, unnoticed and safe.

Artur finally ordered further actions and told his supporters to distribute the leaflets of the organization. Then he sat in Peter's car for a while and talked with him about his plans to launch new websites, and even to establish an underground radio station, somewhere in Belarus.

Exhausted, but inspired by the encouragement of his followers, Artur returned to Vitebsk in the early morning hours where he disappeared in his apartment for the next days.

It was a bleak evening. Outside it was pouring with rain and the water drops were relentlessly pounding against the window pane. Frank felt dull and tired but something inside him still refused to sleep.

'29...30...31', he was counting silently; counting all the men he had killed.

He reckoned up those, he could remember. In Paris, in Sapporo and during the mission in the jungles of Okinawa.

Surely he could still add some more, especially since the Japanese war, when he had often fired at shadows in the darkness, never knowing who had been hit by his bullets. Frank had thrown hand grenades into rooms and trenches, and had no longer checked how many people had been torn to pieces by them.

Meanwhile, they called him a 'hero' but he did not feel like one. A giant burden of guilt and doubt was lying on his soul. He looked out the window and thought about the great warriors of history, those, who were celebrated and honored as heroes in the memory of posterity. Those men with the magnificent shrines and the great monuments.

'How many people may king Leonidas have slain at Thermopylae?' he asked himself and looked thoughtfully at the old tree in front of his window. 'Has he ever thought of them?'

Frank cursed the world in which he was born into. A world in which he had no other choice, as he assured himself.

'I have always been a happy child. Naive and clueless, nonetheless happy. But after a few years, I had to realize in what cruel age fate has thrown me,' he whispered to himself.

'It's not your fault, Frank! You would save every little animal, help every poor old lady across the street. This is you, Frank! A man with a good core. Nevertheless, you have killed so many people...'

Kohlhaas was sitting on his bed, breathing heavily and holding his head. Outside it had become dark.

Two years ago, the new tax administration tax had been introduced by the World Government in all sectors, including 'Eastern Europe'. At that time, a big wave of discontent had shaken Belarus.

Today, on 15.04.2033, the TV stations and newspapers had announced that the hated tax was raised again with over 50%, while the media were trying to tell the people, that it was necessary. Moreover, even a 'great progress'. Medschenko promised to use the money to support an 'improved Scanchip management', but the most Belarusians, who got more and more problems to get along with their low wages, did not believe him.

Therefore, a lot of people were ranting in secret. The strongly indebted sub-sector 'Belarus-Baltic' tried to fill up its empty coffers with this new measure, because the 'Global Bank Trust', the international financial authority, put it increasingly under pressure.

Meanwhile, many Belarusians knew about this and called the tax for administration 'another brazen raid'. The media claimed, however, that more officials were necessary to ensure a better service and a faster processing of Scanchip matters. Nevertheless, most Belarusians knew that the Scanchips were almost exclusively managed by automated computer systems.

Furthermore, the bankrupt sub-sector had no money to hire new officials at all. But what the people thought, was not important for Medschenko and his staff.

From 04.15.2033, every citizen had to pay further 57,99 Globes a month for the new tax.

Nobody could do anything against this deception, because the World Government had already decided it and anyone else had to obey.

Making Contact

'Displeasure is boiling at every street corner!' said Artur with a sardonic undertone, looking at his comrades who had met him in Gorodok.

'Yes, that's right. If you hear people talking, you could think that they will soon go on the streets to protest,' replied one of the men.

'People talk a lot today, and tomorrow they are lethargic again,' moaned Peter Ulljewski.

'But I think, we will become even more popular for many Belarusians. Now we have to improve the structure of our organization and a public campaign has to be started!' said Tschistokjow with a nod.

'You wanted to show us your new 'cell system' today, right?' remarked Igor from Orcha.

'Yes, I will! In the last weeks, I have brooded a lot about the question how we can make our movement more effective and safer. Let me tell you my ideas. We found sub-groups in every important region of Belarus which can operate independently from each other, with only one single leader who is moreover the contact person.

This man will be the only one who has contact to the other groups from outside and to the command. Furthermore, this leader has the only authority and the right to give orders, and he will be the one who gets instructions from the command or directly from me. I will choose the leaders of the local groups in the next days. Apart from this, we can plan actions in secret forums or on our own websites. Anyhow, we will organize our men only in local groups and cells from now on.'

Peter took a laptop out of his rucksack and put it on the table. Artur told more details and his comrades seemed to be keen on his plans.

The blond man added, 'We have to avoid the mistake to allow any so called 'democratic structures' in our organization. This would just be the thing our enemies are waiting for. No! The movement will be build up with a strict military hierarchy - like a revolutionary army.'

'So if group 'X' in city 'Y' is uncovered and smashed by the police, the authorities will have much more problems to find traces to the rest of the organization,' remarked Peter.

Dimitri, a 20 years old man from Slonim, said, 'If we really build up such a big movement, the cops will try to infiltrate our groups with informers.'

'Who is spying for the cops and gets caught by us gets a bullet in his head!' hissed Tschistokjow. 'We have to become tougher. In the last weeks and months, the police had got some internal information, what can only be explained with spies in our ranks. Now it is necessary to keep a sharp eye on our own people. Informers, who tell the cops things for a few Globes, endanger our lives and we will show no mercy on them.'

The other men nodded, Artur stroked through his hair. Then he smiled and continued with the presentation of the new organizational structure.

'All members of the 'Freedom Movement of the Rus' will have to swear by their lives, that they keep silence.'

'And I will ensure that all Rus will stick to these rules, Artur!' replied Peter and clenched his fist.

'What's about weapons?' asked one of the men then.

'It's all in progress. However, I still see no reason to use violence - so far. We will only use it, if the cops openly attack our comrades. Otherwise, we continue to make effective publicity campaigns. We are no guerrillas but want to become a political mass movement one day,' explained Artur.

'Well, all right. In the coming days, we will begin with campaigns across the whole country. The last event has inspired me, we are on the right way,' said Tschistokjow to his followers.

His men murmured their approval and Artur gave instructions for further actions in the bigger cities. They still talked for a while and Artur's fellows really seemed to believe that their small group could start something like a revolution one day. But Tschistokjow, who outwardly looked so determined and strong, had a lot of doubts concerning his political underground struggle.

If he was honest to himself, this all was just ridiculous. But what should he do? He had no other choice than going on fighting against windmills.

'Ha! Great!'

Wilden slapped his thighs and laughed. He almost fell out of his chair.

'Okay, who can read this?' he asked the others after a short moment.

Frank tried to decipher some Cyrillic letters on the screen:

'Attention, citizens! This newspaper...eh...the paper...'

'Attention, citizens! This newspaper is lying to you!' exclaimed Wilden, laughing again.

'True words!' muttered Alfred and drank a sip of beer.

Wilden was amusing himself magnificently. The three men sat in his living room and watched the news on Belarusian television. During last night, some strangers had decorated the white facade of the editorial building of the 'Belorusskaya News Gazeta' in Minsk with a few anti governmental slogans in huge, blood-red letters. Employees of the newspaper hastily tried to whitewash the unpleasant messages, while an excited reporter was talking with a squeaky voice.

'Terrorists? This reporter has said 'terrorists'! What a son of a bitch! Ridiculous! Only because they have smeared a wall, they are terrorists now!' ranted the village boss.

'They talk about this guy again, Artur Tschistokjow. Can you translate it, Thorsten? asked Frank.

The former businessman with the gray temples perked his eyebrows up and tried to follow the rapid chatter of the reporter.

Shortly afterwards he said, 'The police suspects some members of the 'Freedom Movement of the Rus' from Minsk. But they investigate in all directions.'

'Ha, ha!' shouted Alf, scratching his dark beard and fetched another beer out of the fridge.

After the reporter had finished her speech, the police chief of Minsk was interviewed. He admitted, with an embarrassed face that his men did not have a 'hot trace' so far. Then the news showed a huge banner which strangers had attached on a motorway bridge. It was removed by some policemen.

'For an independent Belarus! Medschenko = Exploiter of the workers!' was the text on the banner. Frank, Alf and Wilden started to discuss excitedly.

'A lot has changed in the last few months. Here in Lithuania and in Belarus, many people are more dissatisfied than ever before. Thousands of them are fuming with rage. When I was in Vilnius, three weeks ago, I have noticed the increase of anger when I have talked to some citizens. Raising the tax for administration is another slap in the face of the people,' said Wilden; he raised his forefinger like an university lecturer.

'Yes, a look at our Scanchip accounts tells everything, although they are just fake and we luckily don't have to work for our money. Thank HOK!' remarked Frank.

'Meanwhile, the situation really seems to become desolate. Belarus is poorer than I have already expected it. I'm curious to see when the first riots will break out,' it came from Bäumer, who appeared a bit tipsy now.

'Riots? You can't foresee such things, Alf!' answered Wilden. 'However, I like the organization of this Artur Tschistokjow. In the last days, the media have almost daily reported about the actions of these Rus.'

'We should try to make contact. Maybe we can work together', suggested Frank.

'Hmmm?' muttered Wilden thoughtfully. 'We could do it. Nevertheless, it is very dangerous. We don't know these people and I don't want some GSA agents running through our village tomorrow.'

'I just thought,' returned Frank.

'If we would really contact them, for example on the Internet, we should do it together with HOK because he knows the necessary security measures,' answered Wilden and also took another beer.

'Well, I'm interested in this group too,' said Alf with a grin.

'Damn! Just be careful! This can make us a lot of problems. Let's ask HOK,' meant the former businessman with a serious look.

Three days later, in the last week of April, Frank and Alfred went to HOK, the computer specialist of Ivas. It was noon when they knocked on the door of the dilapidated house in which the talented computer scientist resided, and it took a while until they heard signs of life from the hallway.

'Who's there?' it came from inside.

'It's us! Frank and Alf. Hurry up, buddy!' called Kohlhaas and pounded against a shutter.

'Yes, yes! Calm down, guys!' heard the two visitors. Then the door was opened with a faint creak.

'What's going on, HOK? You have dark circles under your eyes. What has happened?' quipped Alf.

The plump computer expert yawned and blinked at the two men.

'Oh, nothing! I have just played a bit computer for some hours. Can I help you?' answered HOK.

'May we come in?' asked Frank demanding.

'Oh, yes! Sure!' muttered Holger. He went into the house. Frank and Alf followed him. After a brief stay in the kitchen and a few cups of coffee, HOK accompanied them to his office which was traditionally cluttered with all kinds of stuff and numerous boxes. In the middle of the room was a table with a big computer. The two guests told HOK their wishes and the wayward man sullenly promised to help them.

'Okay, but I have to eat something first,' muttered HOK. He went to his kitchen while the hum of the computer became louder.

A few minutes later, HOK jumped into the sea of data, swimming like a happy fish from one illegal website to the next. The world of cyberspace was his element, and once he had entered it he quickly felt well again.

'Look at this! Here they are!' whispered HOK after he had found the website of the freedom movement.

A white flag with a black dragon's head appeared on the screen and the slogan 'Freedom for Belarus!' lit up in big letters. Now, HOK's fingers danced with breathtaking speed over the keyboard. Frank and Alfred were amazed. 'Contact…register…login,' he whispered.

HOK registered on the website and explained, 'I log in from Korea, he, he.'

'Have fun, buddy!' remarked Frank, perking his eyebrows up. Alf grinned.

'Send message!' said HOK silently to himself and a second later the email was on its way.

'Hello,
We are a political group from Lithuania. that also fights against the World Government. Please answer us, so that we can arrange a meeting.'

'Okay, now we'll wait…', said Frank.
'Very good, HOK! Thank you!' answered Alf. 'We will only communicate with this organization from your computer, everything else would be a too high risk.'
'Security on the Internet and elsewhere in the vastness of cyberspace is uncle HOK's specialty.'

The chubby man smiled proudly and finally turned the computer off.

'We go now. Call us, if you have received an answer,' Frank told him. Shortly thereafter, he and Alf left the house.

'Yes, all right!' gasped HOK. He shuffled into the kitchen, ate some bread and read a thick book full of science fiction stories.

The prospect to meet some rebels from the neighboring regions and the thought of working together spurred Frank and Alf to learn more English and Russian. For things like this, there was only one truly competent partner in Ivas, Thorsten Wilden, the village boss.

On the next day, Frank got up early and immediately went to Wilden's house. In addition, there was also Wilden's daughter Julia who Frank wanted to invite for dinner in the next days. Actually, she was even a more important reason to show up at the Wildens.

The leader of the community was proud that his extensive language skills were on demand once more, and immediately started to teach Frank in Russian. After the lesson, they talked for a while.

'I'm not sure, perhaps these Rus are just a bunch of idiots,' said Wilden.

'Well, I don't think so. We will see whether there is a response to our email. What is the worst that could happen?' returned Frank.

'Anyhow, let's wait and see,' said Wilden and waved his young friend nearer. 'Have I already shown you my new library, Frank?'

Kohlhaas shook his head and followed Wilden into an adjoining room which had obviously been renovated only a few weeks ago. Large bookcases were everywhere around him. The gray-haired man rummaged in some boxes that were stuffed with books to the brim. Then he put a few more titles to the others.

'Not bad!' said Frank, still surprised, and gaped.

He had never seen so many books in his whole life because the people of his generation did not read very much anymore.

'If you want to borrow something, you just need to come and ask,' spoke the village boss. 'The books are even ordered by topic. History, politics, economics and so on.'

'That's exactly the right thing for the winter months in Ivas. I will remember your offer. However, when it gets dark that early, I sleep worse,' told Frank.

'Oh? Really?' asked Wilden and was puzzled.

'Yes!' returned his young pupil. 'I think, it's probably the aftereffect of my captivity in the holo cell. Nightmares, sleep disturbances, all that kind of stuff.'

Wilden looked around quizzically. Now he had no longer an appropriate answer.

'You will survive it, my boy!' he just said.

'Where is Julia?' asked Frank then.

'Probably in the living room, with her mother. I have been in the office or in the library all day,' explained Wilden.

'Well, see you tomorrow!' replied Frank. He turned around and went downstairs to find Julia.

He smiled and cleared his throat as the blonde woman came towards him.

'Hi, Frank! I can't believe it - my father has let you go,' joked Julia with a smirk.

'So to speak! He really has a beautiful book realm,' said Kohlhaas, searching desperately for a good topic to talk about.

'Yes, Mom and me see him even more rarely now,' muttered Julia.

'I can imagine. Uh, I must go back home, Alf is waiting. We have to repair something. I just wanted to ask if you would like to visit me for lunch?' remarked Frank.

'Sure! Why not? Nice idea! And when?'

Kohlhaas hesitated while Julia was looking at him with an expectant look; she started to grin.

'On Tuesday. In the evening. I will cook something.'

'Something?'

'Eh, yes...'

'Okay! I will come at 19.00 pm!' answered the daughter of the village boss with amusement and seemed to enjoy Frank's nonplus. Kohlhaas left the house and was glad that she had accepted the invitation.

On the following day, Frank and Alfred visited HOK again. The email had been answered by a 'Sergei'. Presumably, this was not his real name. A little later, they went to Wilden with the printed out message. The village boss fetched a Russian dictionary from the bookshelf and translated the short text. Finally, he read aloud while his younger friends listened eagerly.

'Thank you for your message! We are pleased that you are interested in the 'Freedom Movement of the Rus'. Before we can meet, we ask you for a telephone call. Please call 0131/4458930.

Greetings

Sergej'

A short silence followed. Wilden scratched the back of his head brooding. His guests looked at him quizzically.

'Well, can you establish an untraceable and secure telephone connection for us, HOK?' asked the village boss the computer scientist.

'Of course! This is my standard program,' replied HOK. 'Follow me!'

They went to HOK's house and sat down in his office. Wilden took the phone because his Russian was the best. HOK switched on the speaker.

For half a minute a monotonous hooting echoed through the room, then they heard a voice at the other end of the line.

Wilden immediately started talking at breakneck speed and the two interlocutors exchanged their opinions about some basic things. The village boss did not tell the man at the other end from where he was calling.

After half an hour, they had finally arranged a meeting on 02.05.2033 in Vitebsk. The stranger asked Wilden to call him again in two days to get further information. Then the conversation was over. Wilden briefly summarized the content of the call for the others and looked expectantly at them.

'And? What do you think?' he wanted to know from his fellows.

'Sounds good, Thorsten. I think it would make sense to look for some allies in the neighboring regions. Belarus is not far away from us,' said Alf.

'Maybe you're right, but I'm still uncertain. The name of our village must remain a secret. A top secret, got it?' stressed Wilden with a straight face.

'Yes! Sure!' answered Frank sullenly.

'Who of us will go to the meeting?' asked HOK and stared at his guests.

'I will go! No question!' meant Wilden.

'Yes, and the whole thing is interesting for us too. After all, we are not here for fun,' said Bäumer to Frank and nodded at him.

'Okay, I also want to meet those Belarusians,' remarked Kohlhaas.

'Then we have to wait until they tell us more details,' said Wilden. 'This guy on the phone seemed to be all right - just a first impression.'

Shortly afterwards, the men left HOK's house and went back home. Frank and Alfred were full of expectation, hoping that the meeting, if it would really take place, would not disappoint them.

'I hope that these guys are not just a group of teenage pseudo-revolutionaries,' said Frank.

'I don't think so, because the reports about them on television were very encouraging,' returned Alfred. 'Finally, we will see what happens. If they are idiots, we just walk off and they never see us again.'

The next days passed. Today it was Frank's task to present Julia the promised dinner and he had to show himself from his best side. Moreover, he had finally decided to win her heart, although he was no expert for 'women's stuff' and love was still an unknown territory for him.

Nevertheless, Frank tried everything to please his beautiful guest. He had cooked spaghetti and presented them Julia with a big smile.

'Ah, that looks delicious!' she said and seemed to look forward to her meal.

Frank took a true mountain of noodles out of a steaming pot in the middle of the table and looked shyly at the blonde woman.

'Does it taste good?' he asked a few minutes later.

'Yes, really. Very tasty!' Julia grinned.

Now, Frank filled his plate with noodles too, and immediately started to smack. Shortly afterwards he noticed his loud smacking and cleared his throat. Julia just smiled.

'We can go to Raseiniai, if you like. It is not far from here. There is a cinema,' suggested Frank.

'You're welcome. The main point is that we get out of this boring village. Yes, a good idea. Do you want to watch a specific movie?' she asked.

'Uh, well, yes, don't know. Any film is okay. There is a new film called 'The Slayer - Reign of the Angel of Death'. Seems to be interesting,' murmured Frank.

'What's that for a movie?'

'Eh, nothing, forget it. Probably this film is nothing for you. We should watch another movie, Julia' diverted Frank.

'Sounds like some kind of horror film.'

'Well, maybe with a bit of horror in it...'

'I don't like such movies, Frank. Let's watch something else,' answered Julia.

'Okay! Sure!'

'Where is Alf tonight?' she finally asked.

Frank pondered. 'He is in Steffen de Vries' cafe, together with Sven. I think they want to play cards.'

'Can I have a bit more salt?'

'Yes, of course!'

Frank jumped up immediately and hurried to the cupboard. Then he desperately looked for the salt jar. 'Wait! It must be somewhere here,' he said quietly.

Julia opened her eyes and giggled. 'Yeah, all right! Don't panic! It's not that important...'

'Damn! It is Alf's fault that I can't find this stupid salt jar. That idiot!' growled Frank silently and came back to the kitchen table.

They chatted for a while and he enjoyed the evening with Julia. She apparently liked his spaghetti - more or less.

A few days later, they drove to the cinema in Raseiniai and watched a 'weepie', as Frank called it. But the content of the movie interested him not very much. The main thing was that Julia was sitting next to him. From time to time, Frank looked at the blonde woman with a hasty glance, admiring her beauty.

After the film, she gave him a farewell kiss on the cheek and Frank walked back home with a happy smile and even dreamed of her in this night.

Artur Tschistokjow stared at the screen of his laptop which was illuminating the otherwise dark room.

'Group from Lithuania? Thus...,' he muttered, narrowing his eyes to slits.

'What do you think, Peter?'

'I've never heard of such a group. Sounds strange!' replied his friend suspiciously.

'We have had so many new members in the last months but an entire group has never made contact to us before,' said Tschistokjow quietly.

'Do you really want to meet them? Maybe it's a trap.'

'What's the worst that could happen? Yes, perhaps it is a trap. We are always in danger of being trapped.'

Peter took a deep breath. He was not all too enthusiastic. Then the strong man with the reddish-blond hair answered, 'But most of the new ones come to us after they have been recruited by men we already know. This thing is much more different, Artur.'

'I know. But I think, we should risk it. We need many more supporters, otherwise the movement will always remain on our current level.'

'Okay, then let us meet this group. I will come with you, and some armed men too.'

'No, you'll lead the movement in my place, if it is a trap and they catch me! Got it?' hissed Tschistokjow.

'Don't say such things,' returned Peter testily.

'One of them has called me yesterday, and we have chosen a meeting place. I will tell him now that we confirm.'

A minute later, Artur sent HOK a short email and finally informed the recipient that he was willing to meet him. Then he turned around and looked at his longtime companion.

'You know, my friend, we are following a path that will bring us either victory or death one day. They can catch us every day. I don't want to lead a small group of malcontents. I want to build up a revolutionary mass movement. We have big plans and we have to reach the workers in the factories, the officials and even the policemen. If we want to do this, the eternal game of hide and seek will become more and more difficult anyway. Let's hope that the social situation in this country will bring us the chaos we need. This is our only chance to succeed.'

Peter puffed quietly and twisted his mouth. He did not give an answer and stared vacantly into space. Artur was right, and his best friend knew it.

Conspiratorial Meeting

Frank Kohlhaas, Alfred Bäumer, Thorsten Wilden and two other men from Ivas were waiting on a secluded parking lot. Meanwhile, it was 22.00 pm and it was getting dark. They had driven to the outskirts of Vitebsk in the northwest of Belarus, and had parked their car next to an vacant building. The men peered down a long road which was leading directly to the parking lot.

'Well, it's 22.00 o'clock now. These guys are not punctual,' growled Wilden, staring at his watch.

'I just hope that they are okay, that's the main thing,' said Alf.

Martin Steinbacher, one of the two young men who had accompanied them as an escort, gasped nervously and moaned.

'Stay calm!,' whispered Frank, looking at him and fumbling for his gun which was in the pocket of his coat. 'There! It must be them!'

From a distance, they saw the headlights of a car flashing in the night. Someone was driving in the direction of the meeting place.

'Ah!' said Wilden and became tense.

The vehicle came nearer with a quiet hum. It also seemed to transport five men whose outlines could be recognized behind the car's windows.

Then it finally stopped and a tall, blond man with a gray trench coat got out first. Four other men followed him, looking grimly around. They were dressed completely in black. The blond man came to Wilden after he had correctly identified him as the leader of the five strangers. He shook his hand.

'Menja sawut Artur Tschistokjow,' he said with a smile.

'Priwjet, Thorsten Wilden!' answered the village boss and looked friendly at the Belarusian.

'Could we speak English, Mr. Tschistokjow?' asked Wilden.

Meanwhile, the other men had come closer and introduced themselves too. Frank and Alf had calmed down and welcomed them.

'Speak English? Yes, all right!'

'Thank you, Mr. Tschistokjow!' said Wilden while the blond Belarusian suddenly grinned.

'Tij njemez?' he asked then.

'Da, ja njemez!' replied the village boss, grinning too.

'Choroshow! Then I will try to speak German,' returned the leader of the freedom movement and perked his eyebrows up.

'Good! I'm pleased. You can speak German, Mr. Tschistokjow? I haven't expected that,' remarked Wilden and was amazed.

'I can talk a little bit. It will be enough for a conversation.'

Wilden seemed to like his new interlocutor and started to laugh loudly. Artur's comrades were just silent and stood behind him like statues.

'Why have you learned German?' asked the head of Ivas.

'Well, I'm a big friend of the German culture. So I have learned German as a hobby,' explained Artur, giving Wilden a wink.

'I'm sorry that I must meet you at such a place, but it is because of...safe. Understand?'

'Safety!' said Frank.

'Yes, because of safety!' added the blond man, smiling at him.

The conversation lasted almost two hours and soon it was dark. Finally, only the headlights of the cars gave the ten men some orientation. The visitors from Ivas and their new acquaintances from Belarus were on very good terms with each other and had similar political ideologies. Wilden showed his great world knowledge and was quite amazed that Artur Tschistokjow could answer him on the same level, despite all language difficulties. Deep in the night, the men said goodbye to each other and wanted to drive back home.

'We will stay in contact. I'm looking forward to join forces with you,' said Wilden euphorically and clapped on Tschistokjow's back. Then the meeting was over.

On the trip home, the village boss was effusive and seemed to have found his old zest.

'Tell me, what do you think about him?' he asked the others.

'He seems to be a honest man!' said Frank.

'And he knows about the backgrounds of world politics. This is important today,' remarked Alf.

The two younger men from Ivas nodded and remained silent.

'In Lithuania, there are also some members of Tschistokjow's organization. We will immediately make contact with them. This would be great, right?' said Wilden.

'But we won't exactly tell them where we come from. Even Tschistokjow must not know our home village. You always tell us to keep our mouths shut, Thorsten. And secrecy is the most important thing of all,' replied Frank, trying to cool Wilden down .

'Yes, yes! Of course! We tell them nothing. But I'm just glad to have such an organization in the proximity of Ivas. We can achieve a lot, if we fight together with Tschistokjow and his men.'

'What doesn't mean that we become chatterers!' added Alf and Frank agreed.

They drove through the night and reached Ivas in the early morning hours. Frank and Alfred walked home and immediately went to bed. This day had been exhausting, and now they had to wait and see what would happen next.

Wilden visited HOK several times in the next days and used his encrypted phone connection for long talks with Artur Tschistokjow. The young Belarusian with the amazing knowledge had already fascinated him, and while Frank and Alfred worked in the garden or renovated their house, the village boss just invited his new acquaintances from Belarus - to Ivas!

Wilden had not talked about this with the other villagers and had acted on his own. Soon, Artur Tschistokjow was already on the way to the little Lithuanian village.

'What?' screamed Frank with darting eyes and winced, almost falling from his chair.

'He comes to Ivas?' ranted Alf and banged on the kitchen table.

Wilden made a step back. 'Oh, don't lose your heads. My guts tells me that Artur has a pure heart. I can't imagine that he is an informer.'

41

'You can't imagine? Fuck!' shouted Kohlhaas and briefly thought about smashing his fist in Wilden's face.

'Ivas is a fucking taboo! You have spent years in building up this community, Thorsten. And now, you want to endanger us all just to show those fucking Belarusians your damn books?' roared Bäumer.

'I will take the full responsibility. Eh, and Artur also wants to bring three of his men from Vilnius. For example, the leader of the Lithuanian section...,' explained Wilden and became more and more insecure.

'The full fucking responsibility? We won't have anything from this if the cops come here tomorrow, idiot!' hissed Frank in anger. Then he left the room.

'You bring the hangman to our village. Have you forgotten that the GSA is searching for Tschistokjow?' yelled Alf, standing menacingly in front of the village boss.

'Well, I'm going back home now. Don't worry, nothing will happen,' muttered Wilden and seemed to be offended.

'Damn! Think about your responsibility for all the inhabitants of Ivas, Thorsten!' scolded Frank behind him.

For the rest of the day, Frank and Alfred ranted and cursed because of Wilden's recklessness and his eternal quest for self-glorification. They knew that his behavior could lead to a catastrophe.

However, Artur's visit could not be prevented anymore. The Belarusian came to Ivas, with three other men. Even Igor, a dark-haired man with a beard in the mid thirties, who was introduced to them as the leader of the Vilnius group, was among them. Wilden led his guests through

42

the whole village and spoke proudly about 'his base'. Finally, he started endless discussions with Tschistokjow, showing him some of 'his men' and already promised an intensive cooperation in the name of the other rebels. Frank and Alfred angrily followed him, seething with helpless rage inside.

'This damn monkey!' thought Frank and pierced his gaze in Wilden's back.

The gray-haired man walked forward and led the Belarusian visitors to his house.

'My garden! It's nice, isn't it?' he said with a happy grin.

Now, Mrs. Wilden and Julia appeared at the front door. 'Artur Tschistokjow from Vitebsk and Igor from Vilnius and...,' he explained.

'Anatoly and Leonid!' added the blond man, friendly shaking Mrs. Wilden's and her daughter's hands, and bowing to them.

Julia stared at Frank with an annoyed glance and rolled her eyes.

'If a donkey feels too well, he starts running on ice!' whispered Frank to her in passing. She nodded.

Obviously, Wilden's wife and his daughter were also not all too pleased about the generous invitation of foreign people. Anyway, it had happened. Wilden led them all into the kitchen where a steaming soup and a big cream cake were already waiting for the guests.

They ate in silence. Only Wilden and Artur Tschistokjow talked cheerfully, showing each other how much political background knowledge they had. A while later, they left Mrs. Wilden and Julia and went into Thorsten's new library where the host presented Artur his favorite books.

'This is incredible. These books are more than rare!' marveled Tschistokjow and browsed in an old tome. 'I have the same book, only in Russian.'

Wilden and the leader of the Rus talked for a while about their collections of literature, then Frank finally stepped in and asked, 'Okay, now tell us about your great revolutionary plans, Artur!'

The blond Russian turned around and looked for a suitable answer.

'We have to...eh...one day...make a strike of the workers to start a revolution in Minsk,' he returned.

'Do you have weapons? Guns? Rifles?' questioned Frank, staring at Tschistokjow.

'Not so many,' replied the young dissident.

'Not many?' aped Kohlhaas. 'If we work together with your organization, we want to have a perspective.'

'Yes, you can help us in Lithuania,' answered Artur.

'This may be the next step,', grumbled Wilden who still wanted to show his guest more of his books.

'Next step? Forget it! You are here and you know our village, Artur. Now, we will work together and I just want to know how,' said Frank.

Artur and his comrades looked around, apparently irritated by the angry atmosphere. For a short moment, there was silence in the library. Tschistokjow was disturbed, he stared at the ceiling.

'Tell us about the situation in Belarus, Artur. Is it even realistic that there will ever be an uprising? Are the people really so poor and discontent?' asked Frank.

'Yes, it is getting worse. Fewer and fewer people have no more money, understand?' said the man in the trench coat. 'In Russia are even more poor people.'

'Meanwhile, most people in Europe are poor but nevertheless they wouldn't start a revolution!' remarked Alfred sardonically.

'You have a few hundred men, right?' commented Frank while Artur was browsing his dictionary.

'Yes, hundreds of men. In Russia, in the Ukraine and in the Baltic countries are members of my group,' returned Tschistokjow who slowly became angry because of Frank's doubts concerning the chances of his movement.

'You want to take over the power in Belarus? With a few hundred men?' joked Kohlhaas and grinned cynically. Artur gave him a piercing look, he snarled quietly.

'Yes, maybe...someday...I do not know what will be in the future!' he replied, shaking his head.

'Do you have supporters among the Belarusian policemen and the officials? Or even in the administration?'

'Yes, but not so many..'

Wilden's patience snapped. 'This is a first meeting. We will talk about these things later.'

Frank interrupted him. 'No! We talk about it now, Thorsten! You have brought them to Ivas without asking the rest of us! This was a mortal sin! You have told everyone to keep the mouth shut and now you have been the first one who has broken this iron rule. Your own rule!' scolded Bäumer.

'You have called these guys. Now they are here, in our village! And now I want our new rebel friends to tell us about their great plans to take over Belarus!' added Frank angrily.

Wilden gasped and apparently felt a bit ashamed. His Belarusian guests were silent and looked around in

45

embarrassment. A short and unpleasant silence followed. Frank uttered a curse under his breath.

'Well, then we should talk about my plans,' muttered Artur. 'If you help us, I would be very happy.'

'All right! We go to my office to talk about some things,' grumbled Wilden and waved the rest nearer.

They went upstairs and sat down in Wilden's study. Frank immediately began to ask Tschistokjow further questions. Finally, they talked till the early morning hours. Then the guests went back home.

Frank could hardly sleep for the rest of the night. Questions and concerns were still remaining deep in his mind. Wilden had acted more than imprudent and had endangered the entire community. But a spoken out secret could not be caught anymore to lock it up again. This was a fact. However, Wilden had agreed to support the small gazette of Tschistokjow's political movement with a donation, so that the Rus could increase its circulation. Frank had urged the Belarusians to build up an armed group of members as some kind of security guard. Furthermore, the Rus should infiltrate production complexes in order to organize strikes. Artur had agreed and had promised Frank to work on all this.

For the next weeks, the Rus had planned to spread their propaganda in some bigger cities of Belarus, even in Minsk. The distribution of newspapers and leaflets on a large scale would be done by the younger members of the organization, as Tschistokjow told.

Frank and Alfred, who had already fought in the Japanese war and had killed the governor of 'Central Europe', said to Artur that they would stay away from such 'childish' actions. Moreover, there was a too high risk for them to be caught by the police, if they walked around, spreading illegal pamphlets. Wilden promised, however, to recruit further young people in Ivas to distribute Artur's propaganda. Apart from that, he used the following days to revive several old contacts with some like-minded business partners and colleagues from his earlier days as an entrepreneur. These men would support him with donations as he promised. And the results of his efforts were impressive. Wilden 'organized' several thousand Globes in only a few days.

Frank, Alfred and Tschistokjow were stunned. About a dozen young men from Ivas finally joined the freedom movement, and Wilden's persuasiveness was once again successful.

Sven, the young man, who had returned with severe mutilations from Japan in the last year, led the group and seemed to be glad to have a new task which let him forget his constant depressions.

In the following weeks, the young activists from Ivas were 'on duty' in the north of Belarus, where they spread immense quantities of propaganda material in the rural areas. The result was a hysterical outcry of the Belarusian media which reacted with hate and slander on Tschistokjow's newest 'propaganda crimes'.

The understaffed police in these regions did not came all too often to the sleepy villages and small towns near the northern border. Aside from that, the newspapers and pamphlets were distributed by night, so the Rus hardly saw any policemen on the streets of the small villages.

47

This first action lasted until July 2033. Then Tschistokjow visited Wilden and the others again. This time his best friend, Peter Ulljewski, accompanied him.

'We are planning a rally on 25th July with about 1000 men', said the leader of the Rus. 'In Nowopolozk, near a factory. We are preparing it since one week.'
Wilden cleared his throat. 'A rally? A march through Nowopolozk? Are you insane?'
'Insane?' asked Tschistokjow and scratched his head.
'Insane! Crazy!' answered Alf, tapping his forehead at the Belarusian.
'Ah, yes! No, I'm not crazy. We have many members in Nowopolozk, and the citizens there are very angry because of the government. There are many factories and most of them will be closed at the end of the year. So many citizens will not have anymore work. The production is outsourced to China where the workers are cheaper to pay. Do you understand?'
'I don't know this city at all. However, I have heard that there are some large industrial centers. Maybe the largest in whole Belarus,' said Wilden, looking at the other young men from Ivas who had gathered in his living room.
'All the people in Nowopolozk are angry and very poor. If the factories are closed, many people have no more Globes to live,' said Tschistokjow. His friend Peter nodded, and continued to stare at the wall.
'But you can't simply march through the streets. What's about the police?' asked Frank incredulously.
'The police has only one station in the city. There are not many police officers in Nowopolozk.'

Now Sven intervened, vehemently refusing Artur's crazy plan and trying to calm the others. But the leader of the Rus remained stubborn and returned, 'If we do the demonstration, television and the newspapers will report about us. It will be on TV in whole Belarus.'

Frank laughed scornfully. 'Something like this is nothing but madness! It will end in a disaster!'

Meanwhile, Wilden's eyes were shining and he seemed to have a fancy for Tschistokjow's idea. Apparently, he was under the spell of the young man. The Belarusian finally continued and told further details of his plan. The rally should last only one hour, then his supporters should leave the city and disappear on their own. Shortly afterwards, Peter Ulljewski explained that they would come to Nowopolozk with a few armed men, if more police officers would show up than expected. This all sounded like political frenzy.

After two hours, Frank and Alfred went home, shaking their heads and leaving Artur alone with Wilden and the others. They had enough of the crazy ideas of the Belarusian and promised each other to stay away from all this.

'Do not think that the cops let Artur and his men just walk through the city. He is nuts!' said Frank on the way home.

'Yes, certainly this city in northern Belarus is no fortress of state authority, but I don't believe that we can make our enemies look like fools so easy. It all will end in riots and arrested people. I don't want to waste my health for such a nonsense,' answered Alf and rubbed his dark beard, still brooding.

'Sure! But it seems that Artur wants to attract attention at any cost. He doesn't care about his own life or the lives of his men. Well, maybe I should not say something. I have been not much different from him - some time ago. He is a real fanatic,' remarked Frank.

'There is no doubt. He is a fanatic. Just like you, Frank,' returned Alf and trudged towards the house.

'If you say so, dude. Anyhow, we will stay away from Artur's death rally, okay?'

'I don't intend to participate. Tschistokjow's freedom movement is still far too weak for such a provocative show of force.'

The two men went into the house and talked till the evening. Frank was once more ranting because of Wilden's carelessness and Alf proved him right. But the village boss had already planned another surprise for them.

Two days later, Wilden convened a meeting of all the villagers. Some men and women were still angry because of his behavior, and boycotted Wilden's showmanship by staying at home.

Finally he had announced that all young men had to go to the rally in Nowopolozk. Furthermore, he had already made an agreement with Tschistokjow, as he gruffly explained, and demanded that everybody should follow his orders without asking. Shortly afterwards, a minor riot broke out among the villagers.

'Who do you think you are, Mr. Wilden? You have brought strangers to Ivas what has been more than careless!' screamed an elderly woman.

'She is right! Suddenly some unknown faces walked around here, and no one of us knew who these guys were. Have you lost your mind?' added a bearded man.

John Thorphy, the Irishman, was fuming with rage and was shortly before going for Wilden's throat.

'You have said, no one shall ever know anything about Ivas. And now - this shit!'

Frank and Alfred nodded, mumbling to themselves and whispering to the other villagers. The leader and founder of the community of Ivas was now confronted with the discontent of his fellows and became more and more uncertain. He had not expected so much anger.

'First, you send my son to Japan, and now you let these Rus come to our village,' he heard a woman shouting from the side.

'I have not sent your son to the front! He has volunteered, Mrs. Müller!' barked Wilden back.

'Yes! You have!'

'Quiet, everybody! You can trust me. Have I ever deliberately endangered you? Artur Tschistokjow is an outstanding man and it is furthermore time that we start to fight here! We can't enjoy our hermit lives forever!' hissed Wilden. His daughter, who was standing next to Frank, shook her head.

'My father is nuts, no question.'

'This rally is just crazy. What if some of us are arrested by the police or even shot down? Shall we risk our lives for a ridiculous demonstration in a dilapidated Belarusian city?' shouted one of the villagers.

'I don't think that it will be so dangerous. Our Belarusian friends have professionally planned this rally and after

51

one hour everything will be over, got it? Apart from that, the police presence in Nowopolozk won't be strong.'

'Really? How can you know all this, Thorsten?' complained Alf.

'This is no armed assault on a government building. Just a little demonstration which will attract some attention. Now calm down!' grumbled Wilden. He stroked through his gray hair.

'Anyhow, you haven't asked us, if we want this. And if we want a cooperation with Tschistokjow at all,' said Steffen de Vries, the Belgian.

'Wait a minute! I bought this rotten, formerly abandoned village and built it up! Do not forget that! Without me, there wouldn't be a hiding place for all of you' yelled Wilden in anger.

'Let's see how long this hiding place will still be safe,' said his daughter and looked in Frank's direction.

'But you have not bought us!' growled Frank. 'A leader is only proper in his position, when he shows responsibility for those who are led by him. But you have ignored this rule!'

'Apart from that, you can not force us to follow you to Nowopolozk!' said a woman, waving her hands.

'She is right, dad!' Julia nodded.

Her father looked at her insulted, pushing his thin lower lip upward. For several seconds he hesitated and was silent.

'I fed up with your crazy ideas too, Thorsten!' hissed his wife Agatha in the background.

'Well, I will go to the rally! Who is courageous enough to march through the streets of Nowopolozk for just one hour might contact me. The others can work in their gardens or clean the street in front of their houses! What has become of you? A bunch of cowards?'

Wilden turned around and walked away, loudly cursing and ranting. The meeting was over.

But the former businessman was as stubborn as his new Belarusian friend, and it lasted only a few days until he started a new campaign to convince his fellows to come with him to the rally. Again and again, Wilden talked insistently to the young men of Ivas and did not even stop in front of Frank and Alfred. He stressed the importance of an organized resistance in Lithuania and advertised the 'Freedom Movement of the Rus' as good as he could.

Three long weeks he laid siege to Frank and Alf and finally he succeeded. The two men promised to accompany him to the demonstration in Nowopolozk. Annoyed and tired of the eternal arguing they agreed and gave up.

Rally in Nowopolozk

Artur Tschistokjow had expected about 1000 people to come to his first demonstration, and his followers had drummed up business for the event for weeks. Already in the early afternoon of 26.07.2033, hundreds of people had come to Nowopolozk in order to protest.

Until the beginning of the event at 15.00 pm, finally over 4000 supporters and sympathizers had joined the crowd. Three days before the rally, the local authorities had received a message and had called together all available policemen in the inner city of Nowopolozk. When they saw how many men and women had come out of the trains, and what great number of people was still coming by car, they nervously called for back-up from Vilnius, Minsk and the other cities. It should become an eventful day.

Frank, Alf, Wilden and John, the Irishman, arrived at Nowopolozk at 14.00 pm. Three further cars from Ivas followed them, coming via different access roads to the city, so that they did not form a too long and conspicuous motorcade. The trip to Nowopolozk was uneventful and when they finally reached the city, they could already see a big crowd of people with flags and large banners from a distance.

The policemen, who had taken up position in some side streets, did not dare not intervene so far to avoid an escalation. John Thorphy parked his car near the meeting point and Frank and the others walked fast in the direction of the protesters. Then Artur recognized them, waved them nearer and shook their hands with a big smile.

'Welcome, my friends!' he said. 'I am delighted that you are here. Will more people from Ivas follow you?'

'Some more are on the way...,' answered Wilden briefly and started to grin.

'You have said, however, about 1000 people would come today. But there are many more,' said Frank, looking impressed at the blonde Belarusian and the crowd behind him.

'I did not think that so many people of my organization would come to Nowopolozk,' returned Tschistokjow proudly.

'Don't be too enthusiastic! The number of cops around us seems to increase,' muttered Alf under his breath.

'The whole thing will end at 16:00 pm. Until then, hopefully, there will be just these few cops in the side streets. And they won't do something,' reassured them Wilden.

Frank remained silent for a minute and watched the men and women who had gathered here today. He had never participated in a demonstration and it was, although he had had a lot of excitement in the last years, a great feeling to be part of a protesting crowd like this.

Frank looked forward to shout out his rage about the World Government, despite a subliminal sense of worry that suddenly a legion of heavily armed policemen would show up. Even if he had to shout in Russian, he would shout - at the top of his lungs.

'It's better to mum!' advised Wilden. 'The cops are making photos of us and will evaluate them afterwards.

If they can't hold us back today, they will try to identify and catch us another day.'

Frank, Alf and the others masked themselves with black scarves and put on sunglasses. Furthermore, they wore baseball caps or even balaclavas. Wilden was right, the rally would be filmed and photographed by the security forces who were lurking in the side streets around them. Most of the others had already masked themselves too, as Frank recognized.

Who was clearly identified by the police as a participant of an illegal demonstration, could expect big problems in the near future. However, Artur did not mask himself. His face was already well known, and he had moreover planned to deliver a short speech today. Apart from that, he even wanted to be seen. This rally was supposed to make him and his organization known.

'Have you seen any camera teams or reporters?' asked Frank, looking at Wilden.

'Not yet! But they media won't ignore this. Wait and see, my friend!'

Tschistokjow walked through the crowd and shouted some instructions at his followers. Frank could recognize Peter Ulljewski between a group of young men. He saluted him from afar. The sturdy Russian smiled, pointed at the pistol on his belt and appeared belligerent.

Meanwhile, more and more people came from all sides and Artur started to convoke the clusters of people to from a long line.

'I just hope that we come out of this city again, and everything ends without problems,' said Frank, looking nervously at Wilden.

His green eyes carefully examined the vicinity but it looked like that no further police forces would arrive at Nowopolozk today.

'I think that Artur has planned this rally cannily. The Rus have posted scouts at the major access streets to the city. They will warn us if more cops come from outside. He has at least explained it to me this way,' answered Wilden.

Apparently, he was so impressed by the young Belarusian that he gave him credit for the perfect planning of an illegal demonstration.

Finally, the rally started. A command was yelled and hundreds of men and women started move forward. The men from Ivas remained at the end of the long line of protesters who were marching through the streets of Nowopolozk.

Alongside them were some Belarusians with guns, Tschistokjow's new guardsmen. The leader of the Rus intended to lead his followers from the city center to a densely populated estate of prefabricated houses, about two kilometers away. There he wanted to deliver his speech.

The demonstrators walked slowly through the streets, waving dragon head flags. Someone was shouting slogans through a megaphone. Meanwhile, the 'dragon head' had become the symbol of the freedom movement. It had been designed by Artur Tschistokjow himself. A white flag with a black dragon's head to commemorate the founders of Russia, the 'Varangians' or 'Rus'. The symbol was referring to the dragon heads of their Viking ships.

The marching crowd repeated the slogans with furious screams. It was so loud that Frank's ears were hurting after a while.

'What are they yelling?' he wanted to know from Wilden.

'Freedom for Belarus! Down with Medschenko!' explained the former businessman with a smile.

'Okay!' muttered Frank and looked around.

Shortly thereafter, the men from Ivas joined the shouting and repeated the Russian slogans in a strange sounding gibberish. Then they marched through a rundown shopping center and some citizens hailed them. More and more people came out of their houses and applauded loudly. They laughed and shouted something in Russian. Frank could only understand 'Artur Tschistokjow'. A little later, they turned into another street and marched towards a gray estate of prefabricated houses. Frank saw the outlines of shabby apartment blocks above the heads of the screaming protesters in a distance.

'God bless Ivas! This quarter is more than ugly,' he said to Alf.

'What?' asked Bäumer who could hardly understand his own word.

'Ivas is much more beautiful than this ghetto!' shouted Frank in his ear.

'Yes, you're right!' answered his sturdy friend, looking around in disgust.

The demonstrators stopped yelling while many people opened their windows and screamed something for their part. Some of them even hung out the Belarusian flag or joined the mass. The long worm of men and women had finally reached the second rallying point.

Huge apartment blocks surrounded them now. The mass formed a giant circle while Artur was giving instructions. Frank, Alfred and Wilden made their way through the crowd and walked to the front ranks. The leader of the freedom movement took a bullhorn and started his speech with a booming voice.

'What did he say?' asked Frank the village boss again.

'He has introduced himself to the people as the coming liberator of their country,' said the gray-haired man.

'That's what I call self-esteem...,' answered Kohlhaas.

'What did you say, Frank?' Wilden scratched the back of his head.

'Nothing, it's all right.'

'He promises the people to give them work!' thought Frank. 'This must sound like music in the ears of these poor guys.'

Tschistokjow's voice surged like a hurricane through the streets and he passionately gestured with his hands while his supporters cheered and applauded as loud as they could. Now dozens of people streamed out of their dilapidated apartment blocks and joined the crowd. The impassioned speech of the young politician lasted half an hour and finally ended with a thunderous applause.

Meanwhile, about hundred policemen had gathered at the end of the street. They behaved guardedly and Artur asked them to make the way free for the return march. Some of the Belarusians threatened them with pistols and rifles but the officers just stepped aside and allowed the demonstrators to pass.

'He has said one hour! Now, it's a quarter past four, Artur must end this rally immediately!' ranted Alf.

'Just wait and stay cool! He will end it in the next minutes,' said Wilden annoyed.

The procession of protesters marched slowly back towards the city center and their chants echoed from the walls of the apartment blocks around them.

'Look! The number of cops is increasing,' said Frank and felt his inner tension rising.

As the crowd reached a square with a big fountain in its middle a murmur went through the ranks of the demonstrators and the long human worm suddenly stopped.

A group of policemen had surrounded the area around the square and further officers were waiting in the side streets. Slowly it became uncomfortable. Artur yelled something from the front of the procession and his followers became restless.

'What's up now?' shouted Frank while Wilden grabbed his arm and pulled him back.

'Artur has just said that the rally is over! All shall go home now!' translated by the village boss. 'And he has asked the police to allow his men to leave the city in peace.'

Suddenly, a police officer shouted a response. Tschistokjow answered and greeted him. Meanwhile, Frank tried to look at the front rows and was bouncing nervously up and down.

The crowd finally moved on and reached the police cordon. A police chief shouted some warnings at the protesters, while more and more of his colleagues appeared in the side streets.

'They should let us go. Otherwise, some people will die today!' muttered Alf.

Frank told his comrades from Ivas to prepare for a possible confrontation. Wilden had already become pale. His trip to Nowopolozk seemed not to be as funny as he had thought at first. A group of young Rus roared something at the police, then the situation got out of control. Weapons were drawn and Tschistokjow gave his guardsmen the order to attack the policemen because they were still blocking the way of the demonstrators.

Some shots could be heard and the demonstrators ran forward with loud screams. Frank and the others could hardly stay on top of things in the following chaos. Shouts resounded around them and the outnumbered policemen started to flee. Some of them still fired a few shots at the demonstrators, but finally they withdrew.

Over 4000 people rushed forward, completely disorganized. Some of them ran into the side streets as fast as possible to get away. The men from Ivas struggled through the crowd and tried to identify Artur somewhere in the excited mass, while Frank heard several shots in the distance.

'Let's get away from here, run to the cars!' shouted Wilden nervously and hurried past a group of Rus.

Frank and the others turned into a side street and took their weapons. But there was nobody. Apparently, the policemen had fled and were waiting for reinforcements. Arthur had already disappeared in the crowd and had probably taken a different escape route.

Soon after, Frank, Alf and the others went to their cars and drove away with roaring engines. Behind them, they saw a group of protesters also jumping into their vehicles.

'Damn! These motherfuckers are waiting for us!'

Alf pointed at some policemen, who were standing on the street, excitedly waving their hands.

'Stop! Stop!' they yelled while John Thorphy stepped on the gas.

'Drive on!' shouted Frank at the Irishman who was racing towards the officers with screeching tires.

Wilden tried to keep his head down and was gripped by sheer panic. Meanwhile, Frank had rolled down the window and fired several shots at the cops. One of them collapsed with a loud scream. Then the enraged officers fired back while the car came nearer and nearer.

'Down!' shouted the Irishman.

Two bullets hit the windshield above their heads and shards of glass rained down on them. But the car did not stop and was still dashing straightforward. Suddenly, the police officers jumped to the side with loud screams. Some bullets banged against the rear of the vehicle, while it was speeding across an intersection.

'Shit! We must get out of this damn city now!' grumbled Frank and wiped off some small splinters from his pants.

Wilden fumbled on his DC-Stick with sweaty fingers while John Thorphy hit the gas and drove at breakneck speed across a wide main street, ignoring several red lights.

'Now right, and then there must be a feeder road out of Nowopolozk!' said the former entrepreneur whose nerves were raw.

They finally left the city and drove away as fast as they could. After they had left Nowopolozk behind they came to a larger freeway. Roadblocks had not been set up by the police yet because the most cops were still in the inner city.

'Give it to me!' said Frank and grabbed Alf's assault rifle. He loaded it, while a cold wind whistled through the broken windshield.

'If the cops try to block the road somewhere, I will give them some little gifts - some bullets!' growled Frank, staring at the street.

But nothing happened anymore on that day. Outside of Nowopolozk the local policemen had just been overwhelmed by the situation. They had not had enough time to block any streets or to hold back the protesters.

As Frank later learned, about 200 demonstrators, who had not left the city center in time, had been arrested. Three police officers and about a dozen protesters had been wounded after the rally. All in all, the demonstration had been a success, and the reinforcements had finally come almost two hours too late.

Furthermore, Artur Tschistokjow and the men from Ivas had escaped the police. The leader of the Rus had disappeared in the chaos and some of his supporters had brought him out of Nowopolozk a few days later by night.

'Ha! That was brilliant!' laughed Wilden and enjoyed a sip of vodka.

'Well, I don't know. Artur's demonstration of power has been successful in any case, I have to admit,' returned Frank and looked thoughtfully at the village boss.

'Nevertheless, several protesters have been hurt by the cops!'

'Nobody has dared something like this in the last years. No doubt, it was a great thing. I'm curious what the news will show us,' said Wilden proudly and seemed to feel like a young revolutionary again.

'John is certainly less enthusiastic because of his destroyed windshield,' muttered Frank. 'And his car has some bullet holes too.'

'Oh, the windshield! So what?' said Wilden. 'This is kid stuff. He can repair it.'

'Thank God that he has previously exchanged the license plates. The car has surely been filmed somewhere,' added Frank and switched on the television.

'Don't you think that they can track our way back to Ivas, Thorsten?' worried Alf.

'No, they won't find us. Keep your head, Alf!' answered Wilden and continued drinking.

As expected, the rally in Nowopolozk was the main topic in the evening news. The Belarusian television showed some pictures of masked protesters and also the short gunfight with the police, while the journalists were screaming bloody murder.

Even sub-governor Medschenko expressed his sorrows and pointed out that the authorities would now proceed more decisively against Artur Tschistokjow and his organization.

Finally, the excited reporter went to the police chief of Nowopolozk and demanded an explanation from him because of the deficient preparation of his men. The man just stuttered something in front of the camera and gave the impression, as if his days as police chief of the industrial city were already numbered.

At last, television showed a reward poster of Artur Tschistokjow and asked the people for information where he could be. Frank and the others could not suppress a sardonic grin. This time, apart from the fact that they had taken a huge risk, they had beaten the regime in the sub-sector 'Belarus-Baltic'.

While the media proudly spoke of a 'series of arrests' Frank hoped that all this had been factored in by Tschistokjow, and that the detainees would not tell the police any important things.

But they were wrong. The Belarusian police treated the prisoners with sheer brutality and forced their unfortunate victims to give them a lot of new information about the 'Freedom Movement of the Rus'.

Furthermore, the local officers got support by foreign GSA agents who were mostly successful with their ruthless methods of interrogation. Some of the men they had caught, were never seen again.

Now the authorities knew that Tschistokjow was living somewhere in Vitebsk and scoured the city for him to the last corner. But only Peter Ulljewski and a very small number of Artur's closest friends knew, where the dissident was. Nevertheless, Artur moved to Pinsk, for safety reasons, where a sympathizer of his organization had rented an apartment for him outside the city center.

In the next weeks, Artur came several times to Ivas to work on his Internet presence with HOK's assistance. Wilden and he 'conspired around' and organized one publicity campaign after another, while the young men from Ivas were sent out to Belarus to distribute leaflets.

Meanwhile, the underground newspaper of the freedom movement had almost tripled its circulation. And it was the same with the number of supporters of the organization. The intelligent constructed 'cell system', whereby each local group received only limited information, had saved the organization from major damage yet, although the police was arresting new suspects almost every day.

Meanwhile, Frank and Alfred tried to stay away from any political agitation, leaving it to Wilden and the young people who were eager for new activities after the thrilling rally in Nowopolozk.

Wilden literally flourished in these days, and he soon felt like a true commander. His organizational genius and his comprehensive knowledge helped Tschistokjow in many situations, and when August came to an end, the 'Freedom Movement of the Rus' had become a much more 'punchy' organization.

Moreover, Tschistokjow's men had infiltrated a number of industrial complexes to prepare strikes and to raise the workers against the government.

The group of armed guardsmen for special events and rallies had been restructured and was much better organized now. Even more weapons had been stockpiled.

In addition, the propaganda machine was running at full speed and Wilden was pumping a lot of money into it. A small 'secret service' had lastly been established by Artur and him which kept an eye on suspicious and not trusty members.

Wilden, however, had become some kind of 'PR manager' and reformed the whole propaganda concept of the movement, changing the content of leaflets and newspapers in a way that the mass of the people could understand everything.

'Effective propaganda explains a difficult topic with a few words,' said the village boss.

Besides, he and Tschistokjow wrote a varied program with clear claims and political goals for rebuilding the country and overcoming the social crisis, which had driven countless Belarusians into poverty. Matsumoto's policy partly served them as a model. Moreover, Wilden told his Belarusian friend that the supporters of the freedom movement would need some kind of uniform to give them a recognizable look at demonstrations and rallies.

Finally, they chose gray shirts and black trousers. The symbol of the organization, the black dragon's head on a white background, was designed much more eye-catching, and Wilden even changed the flag of the Rus by adding two red stripes at the top and bottom of it.

In the meantime, Artur had written an open letter that was sent to all police stations in the country in which he apologized for the riot in Nowopolozk, stressing, that his movement would see a brother in every honest Belarusian policeman.

On the new leaflets was basically a photo of him, and he was introduced to the readers as the coming 'liberator of Belarus' - or even as 'last hope for the people'.

It had been Wilden's idea to build up some kind of 'leader cult' around Tschistokjow, because the mass of the people did not identify with abstract political programs but with a single person who represented them.

'An angry crowd is helpless without a man who leads it. It is never able organize itself on its own. Furthermore, it can not be convinced by arguing because crowds are always driven by instincts and emotions. This is the first rule of every revolution!

Moreover, the crowd is not able to think objectively. It thinks only in categories of 'good' or 'evil', 'black' or 'white' and so on. Our propaganda must consider this, if it wants to be successful.

Artur Tschistokjow is always right and good, the World Government is always evil and wrong. This is the first rule of propaganda. A true revolutionary movement does not want to change a wrong system because it can not be changed. It always wants to destroy and replace it! We shall never make compromises and we shall never tolerate a wrong faith.

Our faith is the only true faith! Our truth is the only truth! Therefore, the first principle of a revolutionary movement is, 'Thou shalt have no other gods before me!'

Without considering these maxims, we will fail. They have always been valid and will always be valid,' lectured Wilden.

Artur tried to follow these rules and especially among the young men he found more and more supporters who joined his organization.

The harvest had begun and the young men and women in Ivas had worked for days on the fields around the village in order to take as many fruits from the soil as they could for the winter. Today they were working on the farm of the Westermanns who cultivated potatoes.

'Do you really think that Artur will ever be successful?' asked Frank as he dug out a thick tuber.

'Well, he impresses me. He can talk to the people like a real leader. I would say, he is a born leader,' said Sven and wiped the sweat off his disfigured face.

'Yes, the demonstration has been impressive but it is nothing but a little stitch for the system,' answered Frank soberly.

'I have already been on the road with the other activists, several times, and we have distributed leaflets and so on. Artur has really grown in popularity, even if the media constantly depict him as a madman or even a terrorist,' replied the blond man, who obviously enjoyed it to be a part of Tschistokjow's movement.

'Don't chat about politics - work!' shouted Julia Wilden with a charming smile behind them.

'Yes, darling! We already work hard since hours,' returned Frank and winked at her.

Sven cleared his throat and looked with his remaining eye at him, then he continued, 'When I was in Minsk with the others, we have met some activists from St. Petersburg. In Western Russia are already a few cells of Tschistokjow's organization as they have told us. Believe me, this man spins his threads everywhere and he has a lot of underground contacts in Russia and the Ukraine. He is a genius.'

'I think he is very clever and also courageous but a rebellion always needs a bang. Do you know what I mean?'

'No!' answered Sven.

'It must go a jolt through the masses. An event that upsets everyone. One thing that brings the anger to overflow - a new tax hike or something like that.'

'But millions of people are already very poor. They have hardly a Globe in their pockets anymore. Two months ago, I have been with the others in Minsk. The city is rotting. Thousands of beggars fill the streets. Many people are hungry and find no more jobs,' elucidated Sven.

'Yes, but they have not the courage to stand up because they think that they can't achieve anything alone. And some of them still have enough money to live and they would never take a risk which could ruin their life. Believe me, every rebellion needs an ignition spark. Probably, the time has not come yet", said Frank.

Sven murmured, 'Maybe you're right. But until then, we must preach Artur's ideology to the people. We must give them a new hope, and this hope is called Artur Tschistokjow.'

'Well said, my friend. He also seems to be your hope,' joked Frank, eyeing a rotten potato in his hand.

'Yes, he is!' returned the blond man.

'How do you do, beside that? What's about your depressions? Can you handle them?' Frank suddenly asked and his words pierced into Sven's tender spot. The young man hesitated for some seconds and twisted his mouth. He looked as if someone had simply removed half of his facial skin. His remaining eye turned to Frank and stared at him.

'Well, just look at me, then you have the answer. I am crippled but I try to accept it. I have not fought in Japan, where they have smashed my ass, to give up the fight now, Frank. Apart from this, I have nothing to lose,' opined Sven with a sad face.

'All of us are nothing but outlaws! Some of us have visible wounds, others have crippled souls - like me. You will overcome your pain, and I will overcome mine too. Just visit us in the next days and we'll have a booze. That's a good idea, isn't it?'

'This is always a good idea!' replied Sven, smiling.

Frank clapped him on the back and carried a sack of potatoes into the storage room behind the house of the Westermanns.

Meanwhile, Artur had planned another event in the northwest of Belarus. He had chosen a barely inhabited village near Maladziekna and hoped that the police would not bother them there. Wilden was excited and tried to convince the other villagers once more to come with him to the meeting. Most of the young men from Ivas, and even their families, were eager to follow him.

They had great expectations because Tschistokjow had promised them an unforgettable day. Frank and Alfred were still unsure whether they should go to the meeting. Meanwhile, Wilden's permanent planning, arranging, conspiring and his open cooperation with Artur worried them more and more.

'If the Russians constantly go in and out here, then I'm curious when the first GSA agents will visit us,' said Frank and Alf nodded.

'Wilden only talks about Artur and the coming revolution. If the cops get wind of it, we can ask Matsumoto for asylum one day. Maybe the authorities already know about our sweet little Ivas.'

'If this ever happens, we should hope that we have a revolution tomorrow, even here in Lithuania. Otherwise it could become very uncomfortable,' grumbled Frank.

The two men went into the living room of their shabby house and sat down on the couch. Alf booted up his laptop and examined the website of the freedom movement. Then they watched their latest videos.

Some Russian activists had filmed the demonstration in Nowopolozk and had made something like an own video review. The video had already over 200000 hits.

'Anyway, they are pretty active,' mumbled Alf with a touch of respect.

'Look at this! They spray slogans on walls!'

Frank pointed at the bottom of the screen. Another video showed a group of graffiti sprayers in a foggy night in Minsk. A masked man waved his hand in front of the camera.

'Artur Tschistokjow gives you work and freedom!' translated Alf quietly.

Other videos were about members of the organization with black hoods, distributing leaflets in an estate of prefabricated houses.

Frank grinned. 'For some of these guys it probably seems to be some kind of adventure.'

'But a damn dangerous one,' meant Alf.

'They are daring, these Belarusians. I somehow like it,' said Frank.

Suddenly, someone knocked on the door. The two men startled and ran down the hallway. It was Wilden. Frank rolled his eyes.

The village boss told them with great enthusiasm about the preparations for the next event. Sven and about 20 other young men from Ivas had driven to Minsk to support the Rus. They wanted to stay there for another week, said Wilden, and was proud of the young activists.

'Yes, yes! We will come with you, Thorsten. Please no more lectures,' interrupted him Frank and smiled at the gray-haired man.

'I knew it! Distributing leaflets and spraying on walls is below your level. But this is also a part of our political struggle,' said the former businessman and tried to flatter Frank and Alf.

'We can't be constantly at war - like in Japan. And I'm damn happy about it,' answered Frank soberly.

'If there would ever be one here, I would know where my best soldiers are! You are the elite of my men!'

'Yes, Thorsten. You say it three times a day,' grumbled Alf, perking his eyebrows up.

'I just wanted to annotate...'

'Okay! We will still watch the Rus for a while. If we decide to join Artur's organization one day, we will do our best. You know that!' remarked Frank.

'Sure!' answered Wilden impatiently. 'So you will come with me to the meeting?'

'Hell! Yes!' groaned the two.

The leader of Ivas nodded and turned on his heel. Then he went to the front door, opened it and left the house.

'It will be a great thing! Believe me!' they heard Wilden shout from the end of the street.

'He is the world's biggest gadfly,' moaned Frank.

Great Speeches and New Problems

It was a cold morning and rain was coming from the sky in thin threads. Frank and Alfred reached the village center, where they were already expected by dozens of men and women. Wilden hastened to welcome them. He grinned broadly and waved them nearer. Julia followed him.

'We're ready! You can drive with me!' he said and shook the hands of the two men who still looked tired.

The other villagers went to their cars too. The group of young men from Ivas, which was led by Sven, had already left the village to met Tschistokjow and his comrades.

'I'm really curious about all this,' whispered Frank, following Wilden to his car.

Alf yawned and said that he wanted to make a nap during the trip to Schtewatj.

'At least, Julia is here,' thought Frank and looked at the blonde woman, who also did not seem to be well rested.

Michael Ziegler, a shy young man, who had shirked the military mission in Japan, drove with them. Frank was sitting behind Wilden, together with Julia on the backseat. Finally, they started their trip to Schtewatj where they expected a great event.

'Are you happy to come with us, Julia?' asked Frank.

'We will see,', she muttered. 'My father says, it will be an impressive day.'

'He always says that...,' replied Frank, clapping on Wilden's shoulder.

'You will love it! Artur has mobilized a lot of people!' answered the village boss and started to whistle silently.

His daughter grinned. Meanwhile, Frank gaped at her, preoccupied in thoughts, admiring her long, slender legs; quickly looking out the window again when Julia started to smile at him.

'You seem to like it, don't you, Franky?' she joked and opened her blue eyes.

'Uh, yes, yes! I am already looking forward to the...rally...,' he stammered awkwardly.

'I hope that we won't have as big troubles as in Nowopolozk!' moaned Alf and closed his eyes to doze for a while.

'No, that's unrealistic. This is a quite rural area, far away from any bigger cities. I don't think that the cops will harass us there,' said Wilden confidently.

'Nevertheless, I have a queasy feeling about it,' remarked Julia. Frank had the want to hug her in this moment. But he checked himself and behaved.

'We will protect you, so don't worry' he said then.

She nodded and looked quietly out the window. Frank was bemused and stared at her narrow, red lips which were trembling slightly as the car drove over a paved road.

Her profile was glorious, thought Frank; like a statue from ancient Greece, with an aristocratic, long face, a pointed chin and a well-shaped nose. Julia looked like the prototype of a Nordic goddess.

'Hmmm...,' hummed Frank, beholding her with mouth agape. Suddenly, Julia turned to him.

'What's up?' she asked.

'What? Nothing! I just pondered...about the rally. Let's see how many comrades will...uh...come. Important is that... it is important that all men come...,' explained Frank nervously.

'Yes!' was her short answer.

Wilden's daughter made her lips to a thin, red line and still looked out the window, ignoring Frank. Her father started to whistle again and lectured at this time, for once, not about world politics. But today, he would still have a lot of opportunities to talk about his favorite topic.

The trip to Schtewatj lasted almost seven hours. Sometimes the car drove over ruined streets full of weed which was sprouting between the large cracks and holes in the asphalt.

They drove past Minsk and finally reached an abandoned rural region. Here, the roads were nothing but muddy paths. Eventually, they came to a small village.

Anyway, Frank had somehow enjoyed the trip. He had never been in Julia's proximity for so long and had tried to use the opportunity for longer conversations with her. He had often talked about politics. Wilden, Alf and Michael Ziegler had talked about nothing else too, but the young woman had soon had enough from their revolutionary plans and had tried to find a more interesting topic - without success.

Sometimes Alf had briefly turned around and had grinned ambiguously at his friend. But this trip was not the right occasion to flirt with Julia, especially since her father was the driver of the car. However, Wilden had only one thing on his mind, as always - politics!

The village streets were over and over clogged with people. Hundreds, even thousands of visitors had gathered here, and the fields around the village were full of cars.

'My goodness, what a crowd!' called Wilden and drove the car slowly through a group of friendly smiling men.

'The show starts in one hour,' said Alfred eagerly.

The large number of people almost looked like a small army. Frank rapturously stared at the growing mass around him. Soon after, they parked the car next to a field road and walked to the venue, a large meadow with a big stage. A rock band was playing here and some youths were dancing Pogo and yelled loudly. At some distance, they could see a group of Tschistokjow's guardsmen who wore gray shirts and black trousers.

Apparently the new dress code had already gained acceptance. A few of the uniformed men had rifles and watched out for suspicious people who joined the crowd in front of them. Wilden called Artur on the cellphone and the leader of the Rus came to them after a few minutes. He happily welcomed the Germans and shook their hands with a big smile.

'That's great, isn't it?' he said proudly in German.

Wilden was more than impressed. 'Yes, this is amazing, Artur.'

'Amazing?'

Tschistokjow was puzzled and thought about the meaning of the word.

'This is just great!' explained Frank, still smiling.

'Ah, yes! This is the biggest meeting of our movement so far.'

'How many people have come here today?' asked Wilden.

'I think 8000 people, perhaps even more;' replied Tschistokjow.

'Gosh!' exclaimed Alf enthusiastically.

Artur looked at him quizzically. 'What does this mean again?'

'This is great!' translated Frank with a grin.

'Ha, ha! Yes! Very great, my friends! Today is a big day for our organization,' said the blond man.

Artur finally walked away and went to another group while his friends from Ivas decided to glance around. Some Belarusians eyeballed them carefully. Obviously, not everyone of Artur's men liked foreign guests. But the most of them had nothing against Germans or other people of European descent.

Frank, Alf, Wilden, Julia and Michael soon stood in the middle of the crowd, eyeing the venue a little more closely. Some members of the freedom movement were selling T-shirts and flags at some stalls.

Somewhere, a group of young people was singing a Russian song and the raspy voice of the singer of the rock band could still be heard in the background. It was a tremendous bustle and more and more new guests still came to the little village. Artur could be recognized between some Belarusian activists, looking at his German comrades and waving them nearer.

'This is Viktor from Grodno! He is one of my best men!' explained the leader of the Rus.

A young, athletic man, who probably was in the mid-twenties, bowed politely and shook their hands. He even winked at Julia and said, 'It is nice to meet such a beautiful person today.'

Julia immediately blushed. Frank perked his eyebrows up and gave Viktor an angry look.

'Thanks!' she breathed and smiled at Viktor.

'I must speak with a few other people. See you soon, my friends,' said Tschistokjow and disappeared again.

Viktor remained. He was talking to Julia, in English. She giggled quietly and seemed to be quite impressed by him. The man from Grodno was undoubtedly handsome, Frank had to admit this deep inside. His light brown hair was easily hanging over his steel-blue eyes and his body was tall and thoroughly fit. He looked like an Olympic athlete.

Viktor finally took Julia to the side and told her that he wanted to introduce her to some of his friends. A moment later, she had vanished with him in the crowd. Frank tried to dissemble his feelings but this scenario did not please him at all.

'What does this guy want from her?' he asked himself, turning his head to look at Alf.

'Come on, let's walk around a bit,' said Bäumer while Frank pulled a face. He tried to discover Julia somewhere in the crowd, but he had lost sight of her.

Shortly afterwards, the rock band left the stage and the people moved together. A man in a gray shirt checked the functioning of the speakers, then Tschistokjow went to the microphone.

He was welcomed with a deafening applause, while dragon head banners and Belarus flags were waved. Artur immediately started to speak, in front of over 8000 men and women.

Tschistokjow was not nervous, to the contrary, he beheld the cheering crowd and was sure that his struggle had not

79

been in vain. This event was only a small victory, but a first one, as he thought.

Meanwhile, Frank, Alf and Wilden were standing in the first rank, looking up to the leader of the Rus who delivered his speech with passion.

'You must translate it!' said Frank to Wilden.

'Yes, no problem,' returned the village boss.

Now, Artur spoke with a powerful voice and a loud murmur went through the audience. He introduced himself to the many new supporters of his organization, thanked them for coming and evoked the unity and strength of the Rus.

Then he promised his followers that the Belarusian revolution would come in the near future, and that the traitors in Minsk would soon lose their power. The crowd was clapping.

'He is profoundly persuasive,' remarked Frank and Wilden looked enthusiastically at the stage.

'He is a brilliant speaker! I love listening to him' said the former businessman, gazing in abstraction at the Belarusian.

Tschistokjow attacked the Medschenko government with harsh words and explained his audience its crimes against land and people. He furthermore promised that the old Belarus would be born again one day what his supporters liked to hear.

'This is our land! We don't want any foreign troops here!' Frank could understand.

Again, a thunderous applause surged across the large meadow. The leader of the Rus became more and more enraged, and electrified the crowd like a true propagandist. Men and women were hanging on

Tschistokjow's every word and were cheering even louder. After an hour, the speech was suddenly interrupted by a loud rotor noise. Three police helicopters were circling above their heads and the crowd was shaken by nervousness like a herd of animals. Some guardsmen pointed their guns at the sky and threatened the helicopters which were apparently filming the participants of the event and the parked cars. Artur vigorously called his followers to order, and asked them to ignore the provocation.

Frank ducked and pushed his black cap deeper into his face, then he put on his sunglasses. Hundreds of people around him also began to mum.

'Oh, great. I was already wondering that no cops have noticed all this yet. Such a big event, it is impossible to keep it a secret,' whispered Frank.

'The Belarusian cops won't dare to attack a crowd like this. Not in this rural area. They just film us,' muttered Alf, hiding his face behind a black scarf.

'It is enough if they just collect new information by filming the people and the license plates of our cars. I'm afraid that some of the guys here will be visited in the next days and weeks.'

'Our license plates are just fakes,' said Alf.

'Yes, I know, but I don't think that everyone here has taken the same precautions.'

'Don't worry! The Belarusian cops are just underpaid and listless idiots. This is 'Eastern Europe' - not 'Central Europe'. I'm not afraid of those morons,' remarked Wilden confidently.

After a while, the police helicopters disappeared and Tschistokjow continued his speech with the usual

81

enthusiasm. He called his supporters up not to be intimidated and to remain steadfast in the face of 'regime terror'.

For a further hour, he preached his doctrine to the listeners. Then he finally finished the rally. The singing of an old patriotic song which Tschistokjow had made to the official anthem of his freedom movement, ended the event. The Rus waved their flags, cheered and went back home.

Frank and Alf did not see Artur again for the rest of the day because he had immediately left the place, together with Peter Ulljewsik and some other comrades. When they came back to their car, Julia was already waiting for them. Beside her was Viktor.

The handsome Belarusian said goodbye to the young woman, kissed her hand and finally departed. Frank gave him a black look and got into the car.

'Where have you been all the time?' he grumbled at Julia.

'I was walking around with Viktor and some of his friends. He is so hilarious. Unfortunately, he can only speak English,' she chirped and looked pleased.

'What a pity...,' returned Frank.

'Yes, you should get to know him. He is so funny, and soon he wants to visit us in Ivas.'

'What?' gasped Frank and almost exploded. He could not believe his ears.

'Well, he wants to become acquainted with all of us.'

'He wants what? Good for him!' muttered Frank, staring straight ahead through the windshield.

An endless line of cars was clogging the muddy road in front of them. Now they could only drive at snail's pace. Wilden decided to use the extended break and explained everyone, even those who did not want to hear it, the political importance of today's event. He spoke of the 'growing power of Tschistokjow's movement', the 'revolutionary potential' and the 'cowardly state authority'. Alf saw things differently and started to argue with him. He was suspicious enough to be able to guess that the police had just used another strategy today by filming the rally.

The Rus had openly shown themselves and the helicopter crew had made enough pictures that the police could start a new wave of arrests in the next weeks.

Frank did not care about all this, for now. He felt deeply offended because he had waited for Julia the whole day, like a silly boy. Already now, he found Viktor as sympathetic as a frostbitten toe. Finally, he did not talk with Julia for the rest of the trip, not a single word. Inside he was fuming with rage.

The visitors from Ivas reached their village without any problems because they had avoided to drive on any freeways or important routes. This had indeed taken a lot of time but had finally saved them from police checks. Other participants had been less fortunate. Several dozens of cars had been stopped by the police in the area around Schtewatj and soon the first Rus had found themselves in a giant trap.

The officers had never had the intention to attack over 8000 partly violent and armed supporters of the freedom movement directly. So they had just waited till the crowd had dissolved again to catch one Rus after another on the roads. Smaller groups of cars had been stopped by the officers, and hundreds of men and women had been brought to jail. But this was only the beginning.

While Wilden and Artur still believed that they had beaten the often listless appearing authorities once more, the police finally stroke back - in a way they had never expected.

Meanwhile, GSA agents, partially flown in from the administrative sectors 'Central Europe' and even 'North America', were propelling the Belarusian police and supported them in their fight against political dissidents.

With the numerous car plates, which had been filmed by the police helicopters, many young and inexperienced members of Tschistokjow's organization could be easily identified in the following days.

Shortly afterwards, a wave of house searches and arrests shook whole Belarus. Those, who fell into the nets of the system, were confronted with long interrogations and even torture.

At the end of September, about 50 cell and group leaders had been arrested. All men, who had played major roles in Tschistokjow's organization, had been jailed for a long time. A few had even vanished without a trace.

Because of this unexpected storm Artur fell into a deep hole of depression and anxiety. He no longer left his apartment in Pinsk and avoided any contact to other members of his organization, except for his best friend Peter Ulljewski who occasionally visited him in the middle of the night. Now, the freedom movement had to face a brutal attack and seemed to be totally overwhelmed with the ruthless counter strike of the system. Artur was soon isolated and his organization started to crumble without his leadership.

It Could be Worse

The media in the entire administrative sector 'Eastern Europe' reported almost daily about the latest successes in the 'war on extremists' against Artur Tschistokjow and his followers. In the first week of October, it became even more unpleasant. Apparently, informers had found out much more about the structure of the freedom movement as its leader had believed. Finally, the police even located his secret printing office.

Sub-governor Medschenko took the 'omnipresent terrorist threat' as an opportunity to increase the surveillance in the larger cities of Belarus with more cameras and new scanning machines. Within just one month, the 'Freedom Movement of the Rus' had broken down under the massive pressure. Now it was only a desolate bunch of scared men and women.

All its leaders had successfully been isolated, arrested or even executed. Citizens with secret sympathies for Tschistokjow, who still had jobs and families, retired into private life.

Who had ever been at a meeting of the Rus was now hoping that the authorities had not noticed it, otherwise it meant losing the job, getting a blocked Scanchip or even going to prison.

Even Frank and the other men from Ivas were disturbed and scared. Wilden wailed for days and regretted his careless and arrogant behavior. They could only hope that their contacts to Artur Tschistokjow could not be retraced and that the name of their village would still remain a secret. But the nightmare was not over yet.

'Damn!' cried Frank, almost falling from the chair in his barely furnished living room as he stared in horror at the TV screen.

'Alf! Come here! Hurry up!' he shouted and breathed heavily.

Bäumer sneaked out of the bathroom where he had previously browsed some old magazines. He yawned loudly.

'What's up?' he asked annoyed.

'The city governor of Moghilev, Roman Khazarov, was shot in front of his house in the early morning hours. They say that the killers are members of Artur's movement!'

Alf sat down on the couch, panting, while the shrill voice of the television reporter echoed through the room. She said that three young men had been arrested by the police. Then television showed some pictures of a house search and pamphlets of the 'Freedom Movement of the Rus'.

'Now they have what they need!' moaned Alf and held his head. 'The media will hype the whole thing and the cops will finally have a justification to fight tooth and nail against Tschistokjow's organization.'

'Yes, right,' answered Frank and cursed loudly.

They went to Wilden who had not heard of the incident so far. He had spent the previous part of this day with sorting his books and reacted on the bad news with evident nervousness.

'From now on, as they said on TV, they will put every member of Artur's movement to jail as a terrorist,' told Frank anxiously.

'They would have done it sooner or later anyway - and they already do so, partly. However, now they have a moral justification for such brutal measures,' muttered Wilden thoughtfully.

'How many Rus actually know about Ivas?' asked Alf then, glaring at him.

'Thus, only Artur and his closest fellows,' returned the older man a bit uncertain.

'And Viktor from Grodno! Julia has told him about our village. Moreover, many others probably know about this place because you have talked to them. I know it, Thorsten!' yelled Frank at Wilden.

'Well, I could not imagine that one day...,' stammered the man, trying to find an excuse.

'Shit!' hissed Alf and followed Frank who was leaving the house.

The next days were ruled by anxiety and nervousness, and it was unlikely that it would become better.

'Have you gone insane?' shouted Tschistokjow and his voice echoed from the dark cellar up to the street.

Peter Ulljewski was holding a trembling young man named Martin Malkin, the head of the group of Moghilev, in his strong hands and shook him. Then he pushed him against the gray concrete wall of the room.

'We thought...,' stammered the frightened young activist and gasped for breath.

'Have I allowed this?' ranted Artur.

'No, but...but the cops have shot two of our men. For no reason!' said Malkin sheepishly.

'Hell! Now tell us what has happened in Moghilev?' growled Peter.

'Some of our comrades were in a pub in the inner city, where they got some troubles with a few Azerbaijanis. Meanwhile, they live in the east of Moghilev - en masse!' explained Malkin.

'I know that! Go on!' interrupted him the leader of the Rus.

'Yes, and the conflict heated up. The Azerbaijanis finally waited on the street in front of the pub and drew knives and brass knuckles, it were six of those fucking wogs. Then our men came out of the pub and there was a first fight. One of us was wounded by a knife and the wogs ran away to call their friends. After half an hour, they came back with about 30 further men. Meanwhile, our comrades had also rounded up some other Rus who wanted to help us against that scum.

Shortly afterwards, two police cars arrived and the cops accused our people that they were to blame for the dispute and wanted to instigate riots. Those damn Azerbaijanis could just walk away and the cops didn't touch them!'

'Did the policemen knew that you are members of the freedom movement?' inquired Artur and nervously stroked through his hair.

'No! Of course not! Some of our men were very angry about the behavior of the cops and yelled something at them. Then followed a brief scuffle and the cops suddenly shot around without hesitation. My best friend was hit in the face and died instantly, another was shot in the stomach and bled to death on the street.'

'Yes, and then?' asked Artur.

'I haven't been there. It's just what the others have told me. However, the rest of our men ran away.'

'What has it to do with Khazarov?' screamed Peter from the side and pressed Malkin against the wall.

'Damn! They have killed my best friend Alexander with whom I have grown up. In the following days all of us were fuming with rage. Some of our younger men called for a campaign of revenge. Someone had to pay for all this! Someone who is responsible for all that shit! We had so many problems with the cops and these gangs of foreigners and then...'

'And then you have arranged to gun down the city governor?' shouted Tschistokjow.

'No! Three of our guys have made it on their own.'

'Bloody hell!' grumbled Artur, kicking against a wooden box which burst with a loud crack.

'I should shoot these idiots! Since when are things like that done without my permission? Since when are things like that done at all - by members of my organization? We are freedom fighters, political activists and no terrorists!' hissed the blond man.

'Now they will hunt us down like mangy dogs. Just wait and see,' muttered Peter Ulljewski and turned his back on the others.

Artur's best friend and longtime supporter had correctly assessed the situation. In the following weeks, the media reported almost daily about new arrests. The three young assassins from Moghilev, who had quickly been found by the police, were convicted in a spectacular show trial and finally hanged a few days later. Many ordinary citizens, who had viewed Tschistokjow as some kind of reformer or even liberator, became uncertain now, because the media incessantly presented him as a leader of a 'terrorist gang' or called him the 'most dangerous maniac of Belarus'.

Ultimately, parts of the 'Freedom Movement of the Rus' broke down under the increasing pressure and the structure of the organization started to crumble.

Meanwhile, Artur had been brought to a secret location, somewhere in the north of the country. And he never left his hiding place again.

Apart from that, the inhabitants of Ivas tried to live their lives and hoped that nobody would ever recognize the true character of their village.

In the meantime, Frank sank in a state of lethargy and sadness when the winter of 2033 came over Lithuania and the first snowflakes fell from the sky.

Occasionally, Frank asked Wilden whether he had heard something of Tschistokjow but the village boss always reacted with a shrug of the shoulders. The only positive news came from Japan because Wilden had telephoned with Mr. Taishi from time to time. In the Far East president Matsumoto was building up his country and had consolidated his reign. This was the lone little flicker of hope in these dark days.

But there was one Rus who still came to Ivas. It was not Artur Tschistokjow, who was still hiding somewhere in Belarus, hoping that the storm would die down again. No, it was Viktor, the handsome, athletic leader of the group in Grodno. He visited the Wildens several times on his own. With a special interest for Julia.

Her father found him quite sympathetic, although he was not all too pleased if visitors from the outside still came to the village. His daughter, however, was pleased, very pleased.

She had invited Viktor, just as she had promised it at the rally in Schtewatj. One day, Frank saw them talking and laughing loudly when they walked through the village. He did not believe his eyes.

'What the hell does the pretty boy do here?' he muttered silently, when Julia and Viktor crossed the street.

In the last weeks, Frank had ignored her in annoyance because of her flirt with the Belarusian at the rally in Schtewatj.

'I could ask the guy, if he has heard something from Artur,' he thought angrily. 'But he is certainly not here to talk about politics. Arrogant idiot!'

Julia saw Frank from afar and waved her hand but he only gave her an insincere smile and went into a side street.

'Stupid slut!' he hissed quietly.

The unpleasant situation significantly increased Frank's depressed mood in the coming days and weeks. He spent the winter in his house and rarely visited the Wildens. Soon, Frank had found the alcohol as his new best friend and asked John Throphy to bring him still more beer and vodka from his trips to the neighboring regions.

In the bleak winter nights, Frank's nightmares crawled out of the dark corners of his subconsciousness again. Sometimes, the strange visions, which besieging Frank's skull in the black of night, were bizarre and vague. Occasionally, his parents, his sister or even Nico appeared. Apart from that, a lot of other confusing things distressed his mind. One vision still remained in his memory for many days.

As Frank walked through an unfamiliar city, he saw a long line of people who were chained together. Men in gray shirts were driving them forward, leading them out of the town to a large field. Frank walked along beside the line of people and did not know what to make of it. After a while he had reached the end of the line and suddenly stood in front of a long stone wall.

'Forward! The next!' yelled one of the uniformed men and led some of the people to the wall.

He blindfolded them while his comrades came from behind to help him. Finally, the men in the gray shirts formed a long squad column.

'Fire!' it resounded and a volley mowed down the people in front of the wall.

The dead were pulled away and brought to a huge pit, where countless corpses were already lying. And so it went on. Salvo after salvo broke the silence, but the line of people did not become shorter. Frank looked at the scenario in horror and disgust, but the people, who were standing around him, seemed not to notice him. Suddenly, he heard a familiar voice. Frank turned around and saw Artur Tschistokjow.

'Frank, nice that you have come' said the leader of the Rus.

'What are you doing here?' asked Frank with a trembling voice.

'We have won!' shouted Artur joyfully.

'But what are you doing?' stammered Kohlhaas confusedly.

Tschistokjow clapped him on the shoulder and replied, 'What we do? All that is necessary!'

'I do not understand...' said the young man from Ivas.

'Do not ask so much! Better help us! We have a lot of work to do!", answered the Belarusian.

Artur gave Frank a rifle, then he nodded. Kohlhaas paused and looked at him, still disturbed. An uneasy feeling had gripped his throat and he did not know what to say.

'We have won, Frank! You can be happy! And now, help us!' demanded Tschistokjow.

Another firing command was shouted and the sound of guns followed. Artur disappeared again, leaving Frank alone with his rifle.

The dreamer's eyes opened and Frank held his head. He was clinging to his blanket and looked around.

'Will it all end like this?' he asked himself.

Cold Days

While Alfred was totally drunk at Wilden's New Year's Eve party, Frank stayed at home - alone. Today he was not in celebratory mood at all. Any hope, concerning the political struggle and also his private life, seemed to be lost.

This winter was even harsher and darker than the last. Not only in Frank's soul, but also in reality. A wave of extreme coldness had swept over Russia and the surrounding lands. The Baltic countries had already been buried under a thick layer of snow since the end of February 2034.

In this terrible time, thousands of homeless people and beggars froze or starved to death in the cities of Eastern Europe. And the number of those, who could not afford a roof above their heads and had no more chance to find a job, was still growing. It was similar in large parts of Europe, but the situation in Eastern Europe was even worse. A black cloud of discontent had come over the land and the despair of millions had reached a new scale. In addition, the new year had started with a massive tax hike in order to fill up the ever-empty coffers of the sub-prefecture 'Baltic-Belarus'.

However, a large part of the funds was spent to pay debts and was issued just as quick as it had been taken, while the 'Global Bank Trust', the international fiscal authority, was increasing the pressure on the sector without mercy.

Slowly, Belarus and the Baltic states became a fertile soil for unrest but Tschistokjow seemed to have vanished. He was still hiding somewhere and shunned the public for obvious reasons. Instead, he wrote a book called 'The Way of the Rus' in which he described his political goals. Furthermore, it was also some kind of biography.

In these months, the young politician wrote down his thoughts with feverish passion, and soon his book had more than 1200 pages.

Artur Tschistokjow was willing to come back. The wave of persecution and the brutal destruction of his organization had only temporarily demoralized him, but then his visions of a free Belarus and his fanatical will had returned again, leaving him no longer time to rest. His parents and his older brother had meanwhile been murdered during the last execution campaign of the GSA, after a long time in prison. One of his comrades had told him about the fate of his family. It had happened at the beginning of the year.

Apparently, the authorities had allowed his relatives some kind of last respite before they had finally killed them, because they had hoped that Tschistokjow would leave his hiding place to search for them. But he had not been so stupid, and after a while his parents and his brother had not been useful anymore in the eyes of the GSA.

Artur's hate had grown to the extreme during these winter months, and he had increasingly become aware that his life would only make sense if he would fulfill his political mission. Finally, he built up a rock-solid, fanatic resoluteness to fight with all the consequences. Victory or death. This was Tschistokjow's new credo.

Frank, Alfred, Wilden and Sven were already waiting in HOK's study since half an hour, eagerly longing for the ringing of the phone. This morning, Artur had contacted the computer scientist on a encrypted line and had asked for Wilden. HOK had explained that he needed to get the village boss first, and Tschistokjow had promised that he would call them again at 13.00 pm.

'It is almost March! Where has this guy been all the time?' asked Frank the others.

'Don't ask me such things. But hiding has been the only chance for him. We should be glad that the authorities haven't found a trace so far which has lead them to Ivas,' said Wilden who was staring at the phone.

It was 13.20 pm; the display lit up and a ringing ended the silence.

'Hello?' Wilden took the call with the hidden ID.

'Thorsten, it's me!'

'Ha, ha! You're alive! Where have you been all the time?'

'I was hiding. I will come to Ivas. Tomorrow.'

'Great! We all look forward to see you. When will you come?'

'About 15.00 pm. If it's okay.'

'Sure! See you tomorrow!'

Wilden hung up and happily looked at the others, while Frank let out a cry of joy.

'Thank God, he is still alive!' said Kohlhaas with ease and sat down again.

'If they would have caught him, we would already know it from the media. What do you think?' returned Alf.

'That's certainly true! Damn, I'm just happy,' remarked Frank who rose his fist like an Olympian.

Artur bowed politely and winked at Mrs. Wilden who had opened the door. Then he came up the stairs and entered the office of the village boss where a dozen men welcomed him.

'I'm among the living. Back from exile!' joked the Belarusian.

'Where have you been?' asked Frank.

'Near Khoyniki, in southern Belarus. I thought that the police would not search for me there. They were mostly looking for me in the north.'

'Ha, ha! Peter has organized it, right?' said Wilden and contentedly leaned back in his chair.

'Yes, he and other friends.'

'And now? Will you continue your struggle against the system?' asked Sven.

Artur paused for a few seconds, staring at the men in front of him with a severe look. Then he answered, 'Yes, of course! Now harder than ever!'

He opened his briefcase and took out a huge stack of papers. Then he gave them to Wilden.

'What's that?'

'The manuscript of my book which I have written in the last months. It is called 'The Way of the Rus', my political manifesto. You can read it if you want. One day I will publish it.'

'Sounds good!' added Frank, nodding at Tschistokjow.

'Seems to be very interesting,' murmured Wilden. 'Let's see if my Russian is really that good.'

'The economical crisis is growing in Belarus. It is getting worse,' said Artur.

'Yes, there is probably more potential for us than one year ago,' meant the village boss.

'Right! Even more poor people, more problems in every region of the country.'

'But your organization has been destroyed, hasn't it?' asked a young man in the background.

'It is has not totally been destroyed, some structures are still there, my friends. I will now fight to win. And I will never hide again,' growled Tschistokjow full of bitterness.

'They have said on TV that you have committed suicide, some weeks ago. The report about your death has also been on the English-speaking channels,' said Sven.

'Oh, I haven't noticed this...,' marveled Alf.

'But it is true. I have seen it as well!", returned Frank.

'No, I'm still alive. Suicide? Pah! They lie! They are still lying on television! They have killed my parents and my brother in January. I know it from one of my friends,' hissed Artur and bared his teeth.

Frank inwardly winced when Tschistokjow told this. He knew too well how he was feeling. The same cruel calamity had come over him a few years ago.

'They have arrested my parents and my brother to lure me out of my hiding,' continued Artur.

'Yes! I know what you mean!' whispered Frank, feeling a burning hatred rising inside his mind. 'They have done the same to me! Those fucking rats!'

'This is our 'disaster'...in English,' said Artur with a cynical smile.

'Fate! This is our fate,' answered Frank and nodded approvingly.

'But one day they will pay! If we ever get the power in Belarus, those bastards will pay! I will spill their blood! I swear it!' muttered Artur with staring eyes.

Meanwhile, the situation had calmed down a bit. At least, concerning the immense pressure that the authorities and the GSA had put on the supporters of the Rus in the last six months. Apparently, Medschenko and his staff thought that the organization had completely been destroyed after they had detained thousands of suspects in the whole country. But they had not caught the head of the movement who had become an even more radical and resolute revolutionary than before.

Now, Artur was ready for anything and was not afraid of the thought to be led to the scaffold one day. He knew, deep inside, that a man like him had to make his peace with God early enough before he started to walk the path of resistance against an almighty enemy.

In the first week of March, Artur and Peter made their way to Minsk. In a suburb in the west of the city they had rounded up about hundred members of the organization. It was Tschistokjow's first attempt since months to gather the disoriented men under the banner of the dragon head again. Many had been beside themselves with joy, when they had heard that the rebel leader was active again. Finally, they met in an empty sports hall in the outskirts of the city.

About a dozen men had rifles. They were staring at the rain-wet parking lot in front of the building. If the police would dare to show up today, then some people would die. Artur had already said this to his men, because the new way should be the violent one.

Artur briefly talked with some of the group leaders from the largest city of the sub-sector 'Belarus-Baltic', then Michael Tcherezow, one of the section commanders, went to the speaker's desk at the end of the hall.

After he had welcomed the activists, it was Tschistokjow's turn. The blond man paused some minutes, he stared at his followers with a black look while a fanatic will was taking over his mind. Finally, he started his speech and his pervasive voice slowly became louder.

'My comrades! My friends!
When we started with our struggle, a few years ago, we were nothing but a tiny band of barely 300 men across the whole country. Despaired of the present and driven by sorrows, frustration and distress. We had come from all parts of society with one common goal. We wanted to safe the future of our nation, and make it free and independent again!
Now we are almost destroyed. We have almost been wiped out. They have made us anonymous. The regime has fought us with all its weapons, arrested and murdered our men, inundated us with lies and slander.
They have tried a lot to destroy us - and obviously our name and our symbol have already been enough that they had to use such desperate measures.
In our helplessness we stand up again now. We defend what has perhaps already fallen, and then we go from the defense to a new impetuous attack!
Give us back our freedom! Give us back our country! We will not rest until this system is dead or we are! We have nothing to regret and we will not give up! We will continue our fight! Even with more fanaticism and selflessness as our enemies can imagine!
Their terror just makes us hard. And one day, we will not forgive! We won't give them mercy, as they have never given mercy to us, our entire nation and also to the rest

of the world! It will be a brutal fight till death, and we are ready to carry this burden and to go on! The time for compromises is over!

I have spoken with many of our comrades in the last days. Some had been imprisoned, others had been tortured in order to disclose more information about me. However, some of our brothers had not even had the pleasure to be detained at all, they had been killed immediately. We will see them again, one day, in heaven, and then we can hopefully tell them, 'We have finally won this endless fight, down on earth. Now, our children grow up as free men and women, in a country that belongs to them!

Who is not ready to join this fight to the last bullet shall go now, and may never come back! Who loves his own life more than the life of our nation, shall disappear forever!

All the others may come with me, follow me. Even if I have to lead you through hell. But I know that at the end of this terrible way a new day is waiting for us!

We will not surrender! We will not give up! They have to kill all of us to silence us again! And we will kill all of them too if the balance of power will change one day! There are no more compromises to make, my brothers! All that remains is one single slogan: Victory or death!'

Thunderous applause followed. These were exactly the words, Tschistokjow's men wanted to hear. At least, most of them. A few of his comrades, however, were disturbed because Artur radiated an uncanny resoluteness and a fanatical willpower on this day. His words seemed to sound exaggerated, at first sight, but he was deadly serious.

The leader of the Rus spent the rest of the month with a tireless journey through all the major cities of the country where he summoned his followers, hammering the principles of the new strategy into their heads.

Many of his former comrades had left the organization, but those, who had remained loyal to him, were sworn to the new way with almost insane stubbornness. Tschistokjow wanted to take the gloves off and make his organization to a mass movement. Meanwhile, the economic situation had dramatically deteriorated and now it was time to harvest. However, this harvest should become bloody.

In Ivas life went on as always. Artur's visit had built up the morale of the villagers and Wilden stayed in close contact with the Belarusians. The group of young men under the leadership of Sven, which had supported the Rus in the last months, became once more active and soon all were enthusiastic again. In the rainy April, they started a new publicity campaign with feverish eagerness in Lithuania and Belarus.

Sven's group left Ivas for weeks to help the Belarusian comrades in several cities. But Frank and Alfred still observed Tschistokjow's return to the political stage from the distance.

At the end of April, Artur led a rally through the streets of Brest. About 1000 of his followers came and marched through downtown for an hour. There were heavy clashes with the police and two dozen people were killed. One week later, the men of the freedom movement appeared with about 300 men in Pinsk, in front of a factory in order to encourage the workers to start a strike. Two protest marches followed in Slutsk and Begoml. The media reported nationwide about the re-appearance of Tschistokjow and the authorities stroke back with arrests, interrogations and even executions. This meant that Artur finally ordered his followers to use violence as well. In return, two newspaper editors, who had been loyal to the regime, were shot by masked men on open street in Minsk.

Furthermore, a judge, who had sentenced several Rus to death, was killed by an unknown man a few days later. All in all, many desperate Belarusians were impressed by the courage and resoluteness of Tschistokjow, and the ranks of his movement slowly filled again. His decision to accept the challenge to fight a brutal and completely overpowering system even caused some admiration among the Belarusian policemen. When his men eventually managed to march through three towns simultaneously, the media gave the Rus more attention than ever before. In reverse, Artur publicly shouted out his claims and attacked the Medschenko government with hard words.

Now, tens of thousands of people got to hear unpleasant truths which the media had always kept under wraps. Medschenko and his political staff were openly exposed and their crimes became public. The most Belarusians, who heard Tschistokjow's speeches, started to question the regime and in some parts of the country the television propaganda had more and more problems to convince the people of the evil character of the freedom movement.

Apart from that, the Belarusian industry collapsed in spring 2034 in an dimension nobody had expected before. Tens of thousands of Belarusian workers lost their jobs, whole factory complexes were closed and outsourced to other countries. In return, the food prices and fees continued to increase. A dark cloud of wrath was subliminally pulsing in the minds of many people, and there was no hope that the situation would become better in the next years.

Moreover, a growing number of Belarusians had a violent aversion to the non-European foreigners the Medschenko government had brought into their country. So the tensions between the native Belarusians and the immigrants were increasing, especially in the bigger cities. Criminal gangs from the non-Russian parts of the old Soviet Union, Anatolia or even Africa were still flooding the country and became a talking point because of robbery, murder, drug trafficking and other crimes. Some neighborhoods in the larger cities of Belarus had meanwhile become dangerous ghettos full of poverty, crime and violence. The explosive mood in the country was heating up, inching its way towards a big explosion.

'We're going to demonstrate in every bigger city in the country,' said Artur and took a sip of tea.

Today they had met in Frank's house. Wilden was also there and had brought a map of Belarus. Warm sun rays came through the kitchen window and lit up the still dilapidated room in a pleasant light.

'And you want to hold a rally here?' asked Frank, pointing his finger at Verkhnedvinsk, a small town near the Lithuanian border.

'Yes, I start in the north of Belarus and then I go to the south till the border of the Ukraine,' explained the leader of the Rus confidently.

'But then the authorities will always know, where you will appear next...,' said Alf, still puzzled.

'What's about Minsk?' asked Frank.

'They shall know it, no more hiding. In the small towns are only a few policemen and we will be more and more people. Then there will be a confrontation! So what?' remarked Artur grimly.

'And Minsk?' returned Frank.

'We will not demonstrate in Minsk. It's too dangerous! Not even in the other bigger cities, such as Vitebsk, Gomel and so on.'

Artur explained further details of his plan. He wanted to challenge the system at first in the rural regions. Wilden liked the idea and praised the resoluteness of the young politician. Nevertheless, Frank and Alfred were not completely convinced of Artur's ideas.

On 05.03.2034, the Rus started with a first protest march in Verkhnedvinsk, a sleepy little town with barely 15000 inhabitants in the north of Belarus. About 2000 men could be rounded up by Tschistokjow who delivered a speech which lasted for over two hours.

The response of the population was enormous and Artur was welcomed by many people as a liberator, while the small number of policemen abstained from attacking the protesters and just filmed the rally from the distance. This was an initial success. One week later, the Rus marched through the streets of Disna. Sven and the other young people from Ivas had distributed thousands of leaflets around the town and had earned a lot of sympathies from the farmer's families who were fighting for their livelihood here. Finally, a rally with over 800 people followed. Frank and Alfred were also there this time. Again, everything went smoothly because the few policemen avoided another confrontation with the Rus.

Two weeks later followed demonstrations in Kobylnik and Dokshitsky in the northwest of the country. The rallies took place simultaneously and one of them was led by Tschistokjow himself, while the other had been organized by Michael Tcherezov from Minsk. A total of 5000 people had come to both events.

In Kobylink it finally came to a first clash with two squadrons of the regional police. An officer and three demonstrators were shot, dozens of protesters and policemen were wounded. Furthermore, some Rus were arrested this time.

At the beginning of June, Tschistokjow made a last demonstration in Lepel, a rundown town in the south of Vitebsk. Frank and Alfred accompanied the march of about 1000 men and women as armed guardsmen. It all went quiet and the Rus earned much sympathy from the inhabitants of the city. After this event, Artur disappeared for some weeks and continued to work on the inner structure of his organization.

Occasionally, he came to Ivas and discussed various things with Wilden. Meanwhile, the restless Belarusian had found a new printing office for his newspaper.

Apart from that, Tschistokjow's movement had recovered during the last months and was growing again. All new members were now definitely obliged to appear at meetings and rallies with gray shirts and black trousers - to demonstrate the unity of the Rus. Finally, Tschistokjow even published his book 'The Way of the Rus' which he had written during the winter months.

He sold it not only to his followers, but also sent to thousands of senior officials, police chiefs and high rank administrators to give them a closer look on his worldview. The media immediately reacted on the campaign and warned the people about Tschistokjow's 'delusions' and his 'poor piece of workmanship, full of hate speech and deceitful propaganda'. Nevertheless, he had some success. During the next rally in the small border town of Surazh, some of the police officers, who observed the march of over 4000 demonstrators, were unusually friendly and behaved conspicuously courteous. Even Frank and Alfred were impressed by the bold appearance of their Belarusian comrades and flanked the crowd again as armed guardsmen. One day, as they hoped, also a part of the underpaid and frustrated Belarusian policemen would join their movement.

Special Forces Frank

'Slowly everything takes shape,' said Frank with a smile and turned to Alf. Bäumer took another sip of cold lemonade, agreed without saying a word and looked across the square in the middle of Ivas.

'Do you want to have another baguette?' they heard from behind.

'Yes, please!' answered Frank.

It was Steffen de Vries, the Belgian. Today, the two men were sitting in the only cafe of their village. Steffen de Vries, the sprightly Fleming, had opened it last month. The chubby man had converted one of the empty shops in the center of the village into a makeshift cafe. Next to them there was another shop in which the Belgian with the reddish beard and the big cheeks sold all sorts of useful things.

Steffen gave Frank a small plate with a salami baguette on it. Kohlhaas expectantly opened his eyes. Then he almost devoured the delicious food like a hungry python.

'You have become a real entrepreneur, right?' he said, loudly smacking .

'Yes, the cafe has been a good idea, hasn't it?' answered de Vries.

'Does it run?' joked Alf.

'Well, the Dreher family has already been here today. With their four children,' retorted the Fleming grinning.

'Better than nothing,' remarked Frank.

'I won't become a millionaire, but I like my job,' added Steffen and disappeared again.

Frank's eyes wandered across the village square. Weed was sprouting between the cobblestones out of every crack. The old church, opposite the cafe, had still more fallen into ruin in the last years and the memorial stone in the middle of the square was still overgrown with all sorts of scrub.

'We should clean up a little bit here, and whip our village into shape,' said Frank.

'Yes, you can suggest it to Wilden,' replied Alf.

'Too bad that the church is crumbling, actually it's a beautiful building. Perhaps we should restore it,' commented Frank.

'Hardly anyone in Ivas needs an old church!'

'We could make a nice meeting room of it. What do you think?'

'Okay, if you like...'

'I will speak with Thorsten. It hurts me somehow that an old building is just rotting in front of us. The church doesn't deserve such a fate.'

Alf looked puzzled. 'Church? Fate? You probably become a bit sentimental now, dude.'

'No, but I respect old buildings,' replied Frank sullenly, feeling misunderstood.

'Wow! Look at this!'

Alf suddenly pointed towards the other end of the village square. Julia and another person came in sight.

A few seconds later, Frank could recognize, who holding the hand of Wilden's pretty daughter, walking across the square with a big smile. It was Viktor, the handsome Belarusian from Grodno.

'What is he doing here?' growled Kohlhaas.

'Can't you see it? He seems to have visited Miss Wilden,' answered Alf, raising his eyebrows.

'Bloody hell!' muttered Frank quietly. 'Do you think they are a couple now?'

'You can go and ask them...'

'Fuck you, idiot! I don't want to talk to this arrogant slut and her new lover. She can kiss my ass! I don't care about her anymore!'

'What I hear from you sounds different,' said Alf.

'Shut up!'

'You haven't given Julia the time of the day in the last months. Maybe this has been a mistake,' remarked Bäumer and raised his forefinger.

'What was a damn mistake? I won't run after her!' ranted Frank, clutching to the tablecloth.

'Maybe it would have been better if you have done it, Frank.'

'Maybe what? Maybe women are stupid? Yes, could be.'

Julia and Viktor walked past them, waving their hands happily. Then they disappeared behind the old church. Frank called Steffen deVries and paid the price for three baguettes and two glasses of lemonade with his fake Scanchip. Alf paid too, and followed his angry friend. Now, even the comforting warm weather could not exhilarate Frank anymore.

A few days later, Frank and Alf decided to spend more time with supporting Tschistokjow's movement. They even promised Wilden to take part in all protest marches, rallies and meetings from now on.

Furthermore, Frank made Wilden the suggestion to renovate the old church to make it to some kind of meeting place for the village community. The former businessman agreed to the idea and several dozen men and women started to clean up the little square and to remove the weed. Finally, they even restored the dilapidated church. They piled up a big mountain of rubble and rubbish in front of the building and repaired the roof. At the end of the month, they had done a lot of renovation work and eventually started to face the walls of the church with wooden panels. The old pictures and sculptures inside were cleaned and freed from dust. Frank was always taken by a tang of awe when he looked at them.

In September, they were visited by Artur and his friend Peter again. Wilden had told the Belarusians in a longer conversation that Frank and Alfred had meanwhile decided to serve the freedom movement as full members. Shortly afterwards, Tschistokjow immediately asked to talk to them in person.

Frank opened the door with surprise and let Artur and Peter in. The blond Belarusian was grinning from ear to ear while Frank was puzzled. Even Peter Ulljewski could not resist a grin. Then Alf appeared and welcomed the two guests.
'So you want to become activists in our movement now?' asked Tschistokjow and sat down on the couch.
'Yes, we want!'', answered Frank, looking at Artur who still had this strange grin on his face.
'You two...,' said the blonde Belarusian, winking at them.
'What's up?' Alf shook his head blankly.

'Special Forces Frank and Special Forces Alfred, ha, ha!' laughed Tschistokjow, slapping his thighs.

'What?'

'We can really use you!' Artur winked at them again, while Peter nudged him with his elbow.

'Special Forces?'

'Ha, ha! Yes! I know everything. You have killed Wechsler and the GCF leader on Okinawa. Great!' said Artur with utter enthusiasm.

Frank rolled his eyes and moaned, 'Why can't Wilden just shut up? Just one time!'

'Thorsten has told me everything. Damn! You are true heroes!' said the Belarusian full of excitement.

'Damn! We have told Wilden to keep his mouth shut. It's always the same with him,' grouched Alf.

'You can trust me, don't worry!' laughed Tschistokjow.

'I know, but nevertheless. We asked Wilden not to talk about all these things,' grumbled Frank.

'Well, I have asked him about you and he has told me everything. You are real heroes! Heroes!' answered Artur reverently, stood up and clapped Frank and Alf on the shoulders.

Finally, the two 'heroes' reacted a little perplexed and Frank proudly smiled for a second.

'You could lead my guardsmen. What do you think?' suggested Tschistokjow. 'That would be the right job for you.'

'We will think about your offer, Artur. Anyhow, thanks!' muttered Alfred.

The Belarusian did not give up and tried to convince them at any cost. Soon he behaved like Wilden. Frank and Alfred finally agreed and were quite flattered by this offer deep inside. Then they talked with Tschistokjow about the details and were more than amazed, when he explained that he had already built up a bigger group of armed guardsmen.

Artur had meanwhile planned another rally in Baranovichi. He expected about 6000 people. However, clashes with the police were also realistic, because Baranovichi was no more small town in a rural area and not far from Minsk. This would be a real provocation for the Medschenko government.

In this city, a lot of factories and production complexes stood before their closure and accordingly there was a big mass of dissatisfied men and women. The rally would be a similar show of force like the march through Nowopolozk, as the Rus thought. Tschistokjow did not even try to keep any secrecy and called the people up to join the demonstration on 28.09.2034 at 15.00 pm at the town square in the city center. Even Wilden had no good feeling this time.

The media reacted immediately and spread the news of the planned protest march through Baranovichi to the last corner of the administrative sector 'Eastern Europe'. Now, Tschistokjow was expecting a massive police presence and he told his followers to arm themselves and to prepare for bloody street fights. Finally, he even proclaimed that the time was ripe for the march on Minsk.

But in the end, it came different. Already at 13.00 pm, almost 5000 demonstrators had gathered in the inner city of Baranovichi, and some hundreds of them had guns, rifles or other weapons. A sea of dragon head flags filled the town square, and every minute more protesters came out of the side streets.

Frank, Alfred, Wilden and the others from Ivas had come much earlier to Baranovichi to get an overview of the situation. And what they saw was strange - there were only a few policemen.

'Something is wrong here,' said Wilden, looking at the crumbling buildings around him.

'I hope that it all doesn't end in a bloodbath,' answered Frank and left his friends to search for Artur.

Alf followed him. After a few minutes they had found Tschistokjow in a throng of mummed people. The leader of the Rus smiled at them and waved them nearer.

'Ah, Frank and Alfred! You can have a window place today,' he joked.

Then, Artur took a long look at the two Germans. Both had shouldered their rifles and were completely clothed after the dress code, gray shirts and black trousers, just as Tschistokjow wanted it.

'This is Olaf, he is the head of the group of Baranovichi,' said the rebel leader and pointed at a man next to him.

'Hello, I' m Frank!'

'Olaf!' muttered the Belarusian, staring straight ahead.

'There are just a few cops here. I can't understand this,' remarked Alf puzzledly and shrugged his shoulders.

'I do not know, maybe they are scared of us,' replied Artur with a grin.

He stroked through his sweaty blond hair. Then he shouted an order at some young men and disappeared in the crowd again.

At 15.00 pm, the protest march started. Large banners with slogans like 'Artur Tschistokjow - Now!' or 'Jobs and freedom for all Belarusians!' were carried by the men in the front row.

Wilden and the rest of the men from Ivas stayed in the rear of the demonstration, while Sven and his men flanked the marching crowd as guardsmen. Frank, who was walking behind Tschistokjow, tried to estimate how many people had come today. About 6000 people, maybe even 8000 or more. It was a long human worm which was crawling through the streets of Baranovichi.

Behind Frank, the Belarusian comrades were yelling their slogans at the top of their lungs. Artur was silent, however, because he had to spare his voice for the following speech.

Frank and Alf remained quiet too, watching out for policemen and other dangers.

'Where are the cops? This isn't normal. Everyone knows that we are here,' mused Frank and craned his head upwards.

They marched about two kilometers through downtown, passing a lot of cheering citizens and many dilapidated houses. However, not every inhabitant of the city was well-disposed towards them. A few even shouted 'Murderer! Murderer!' out the windows and meant Tschistokjow.

At a street corner, a group of young foreigners threw stones at the demonstrators and finally ran away when they came closer.

Apparently, the media campaign against the freedom movement had already born fruits in some parts of the population. The last rallies, which had exclusively been in rural areas and small towns, had been unspectacular. But here in Baranovichi the atmosphere was sometimes unpleasant. In the larger cities, especially in Minsk, the Rus had to take into account not only clashes with the police but also with some incited people or hostile foreigners.

Nevertheless, this demonstration looked impressive because of the great number of protesters, the countless flags and the uniformed guardsmen and members. Finally, the crowd stopped on a large square and Artur prepared himself for his speech.

Gray apartment blocks and abandoned stores surrounded them here. Now, several hundred cheering people came out of the side streets and joined the rally. They were excited to hear the meanwhile well-known dissident with their own ears.

'Something is wrong here. Where the hell are the cops?' whispered Frank, staring at Alf, who was standing a few meters behind Tschistokjow. The tall German scratched the back of his head.

'You're right. This is absolutely strange. I have expected thousands of cops, anti-riot squads and so on...,' returned Alf, looking uneasy.

'I start with my speech now!' said Artur to them.

The crowd started to form a circle around him. Meanwhile, the whole square, including the side streets, were completely packed with people.

'Damn! It must be a trap. I have a very bad vibe about this,' said Frank and was gripped by a wave of nervousness.

'What shall happen? The cops won't attack us, Frank. Just look at this mass of people,' calmed him Alfred.

Tschistokjow's voice shook the crowd and a murmur went through it. His supporters were waving their flags and banners. Artur, wearing a black leather coat this time, shouted his political passion and all his inner rage into the microphone and began with the usual accusations against the World Government and its political representatives in Belarus.

At the same, time Frank was searching the area around him for possible clues of hidden dangers with the instinct of a hunter. But he could not see very much, because he was surrounded by countless people. So his only chance was to look up.

On the one hand, the constant peering was his job as an armed guardsman, and on the other his instinct told him that something unexpected would happen today. Frank narrowed his eyes to slits and beheld the roofs of the houses which surrounded the square. Again and again, he turned around, although he did not know what he was looking for.

'What are you doing?' asked Alf and shook his head.

'Oh, I'm just looking around.'

'Are you waiting for some Skydragons? That's just ridiculous,' said Alf sardonically.

Meanwhile, Artur seemed to be in ecstasy and was hammering his political claims into the heads of his followers. Frank could understand a lot of the Russian speech. His continuous lessons with Wilden had not been in vain, he thought.

He turned his gaze back to the houses that surrounded the square, while some evil forebodings were rumbling in his belly. Frank was sure that something was wrong.

'They have set a trap for us. I feel it...,' he said quietly to himself.

'What?' shouted Alf into his ear.

'Nothing, forget it!'

Then, Artur's impassioned speech finally came to an end and screams and clapping came from everywhere. The leader of the Rus traditionally intoned the song 'My Belarus', which was always sung at the end of a rally. A loud singing resounded out of the throats of thousands of people. At that moment, the mass floated on a wave of emotions and even the most guardsmen were completely lost in thoughts, singing the lovely old folk song.

Only Frank seemed to worry and was still staring at the roofs of the houses. Suddenly, he recognized something strange in the corner of his eye.

A small, dark spot had moved on a rooftop and had then disappeared behind a long chimney. Frank's gaze had followed the spot and was now trying to find it again. Shortly afterwards, he could see a tiny, black line next to the chimney.

'The barrel of a rifle!' it flashed through his mind.

Now the dark spot was moving again. It was a man who was lurking there on the roof. The adrenaline rushed through Frank's body and he knew instinctively what to do.

With a long leap he jumped on Tschistokjow and pushed him aside. Just at that moment, a bullet hissed only a few centimeters past the head of the Belarusian. The blond man fell to the ground because of Frank's massive impetus, while some Russians jumped to the side. Two more bullets followed and hit the asphalt behind Tschistokjow. A third projectile hit Frank in the left lower leg and he screamed in pain.

With a distorted face he crawled behind the human wall to find cover. The people around him scattered in panic.

'There is a sniper on a roof! Sniper! Sniper!' yelled Frank, pointing at the sky.

Meanwhile, some guardsmen had also noticed the man on the roof and fired with their assault rifles in the direction of the house. But the sniper had disappeared in a flash and soon he was too far away to be pursued anymore.

Alf made a beeline for Frank. 'Are you okay?'

'Yes, I think. I have been hit in the lower leg. Don't worry.,' moaned Kohlhaas.

Artur slowly stood up again. He looked like being struck by lightning and was completely speechless with terror.

Wilden, Sven, Peter Ulljewski and other confidants of Artur struggled through the crowd and were totally confused. Only because of Frank's wariness Tschistokjow had survived this assassination attempt.

Artur had always foreseen an incident like this, but when it happened he had been completely stunned. It had been the worst shock of his whole life so far. During the rest of the day there were several riots in Baranovichi.

Hundred of young Belarusians thought that they had to avenge the assassination attempt on their leader. So they started a witch-hunt on the few policemen in the city, killing two of them and throwing Molotov cocktails into an administration building. The men from Ivas left Baranovichi as fast as they could and reached their home village unharmed in the end. Except for Frank who had a bullet in his lower leg. Kohlhaas could not be brought to a regular hospital and had to be doctored with primitive methods. Finally, Alf cut out the projectile with a knife and disinfected the wound with alcohol.

Limping and Hoping

Frank had to rest for the next weeks. At the end of October he could finally leave the sickbed and was more or less able to walk again. During this time, he was visited by most of the villagers who congratulated him on his latest achievement. Of course also Tschistokjow, who had slowly overcome the shock, came to Ivas and thanked Frank wholeheartedly that he had saved his life. From now on, the two men had a special friendship.

Julia visited Frank too and was very concerned about him. She brought him flowers, books and once even a homemade cake. Frank was inwardly pleased about her care, but he tried to show not too much of his happiness because he was still huffy and Julia should know it. So he remained sober and taciturn. Moreover, he had the wildest theories on his mind about her and Viktor.

Frank had focused his thoughts only on the political struggle in Lithuania and Belarus, and had just forgotten the world beyond.

Only now, when he was lying in bed, after Alf had put the TV in his bedroom, scary things showed up in the distance. The approximately 300 channels from around the world, which Frank could receive, gave him more or less an idea how the future in 'Eastern Europe' would look like.

The World Government was already trying to register the population of North America with the new implantation Scanchips since one year. Meanwhile, the old Scanchip had been replaced by tiny electronic implants that could fulfill all its functions. These new markers were the final step towards the total control of the masses, and the media enthusiastically praised the new improved implantation Scanchip as 'the greatest technical achievement of the 21th century'.

In 'Central Europe', the first mass registrations had also begun several months ago and the global media machinery had started a huge publicity campaign to get the consent and the goodwill of the people.

But the propaganda did not always have the desired effect. Large parts of the population of North America and Western Europe did not join the registrations voluntarily and there had already been riots and protests in the bigger cities. Moreover, the World Government did not want to take too drastic measures against the protesters and tried to 'convince' the population of the new, improved Scanchip.

The worldwide registration process would last many years. Step by step, piece by piece; as the powerful men in the background had planned it.

Nevertheless, during the first half of the year 2034 over 73 million people in North America had already been registered with implanted Scanchips. The first registrations in the administrative sector 'Eastern Europe' were planned for January 2035. Then, also the population of Russia, Belarus and all the other countries should become a flock of marked lambs - under the command of the 'chosen few'.

Occasionally, the first propaganda reports came on television in order to psychologically prepare the population for the coming registration.

Meanwhile, Artur continued with his activities, holding

further rallies, for example in Pastavy, with about 1500 participants. This time, the police was well prepared and threatened the protesters with hundreds of armored men and even three anti-riot tanks. Finally, the Rus had to cancel the demonstration before it came to serious conflicts with the security forces. Nevertheless, several activists died on that day before they could leave the town again. Pastavy sank into chaos for several hours.

Tschistokjow's bodyguards and guardsmen, including Alf and Sven, had to shoot their way through a large number of policemen while the leader of the Rus escaped from the city in a breakneck action. After this rally, another wave of arrests shook the whole country and Artur had to hide again. But he did not stop his fight and already planned further marches and rallies.

In the meantime, Frank was able to walk again and was eager to be active for the freedom movement as soon as possible.

'In one week, we'll be in Krychaw. Do you really want to come with us? I mean, your leg...,' said Alf and gave Frank some painkillers.

'Yeah, I think so,' moaned Kohlhaas and straightened up. Then he limped into the kitchen and sat down at the table.

'Drink something!' said Alf, giving him a cup of hot herbal tea.

'The rally in Pastavy was a mess, wasn't it?' remarked Frank, holding his lower leg.

'Damn! Yes, it was a disaster. After we had gathered in the center of the town the cops immediately attacked us. They came from everywhere and didn't hesitate to gun us down. They even had three of these anti-riot tanks with heavy machine guns.'

'This just shows that they take us serious now. Artur is still alive and now they try to stop us with sheer brutality,' returned Frank.

'Remember the sniper! It was the GSA! It wasn't the ordinary Belarusian police, I'm sure about that.'

'We will never know it, Alf. Anyhow, I have seen a report on ANN yesterday, this American channel. Millions of people in North America have already been registered with the new implanted Scanchips. Wilden says there are hidden nano poison capsules inside these fucking things. Those, who have been registered, can be 'switched off' by pressing a button. The poison capsule can be activated with radio waves or something like that.'

'Nobody will ever implant me such a chip! Over my dead body!' growled Alf and clenched his fists in rage.

'But a great number of people has already been chipped. They believe the lies of the media. Stupid lambs..'

'What's about 'Eastern Europe'?' asked Bäumer full of sorrow.

'Probably the first registrations will start here next year!' explained Frank.

'If they ever register us with these fucking things, we are all finished!'

'Well, we still have some time, Alf. At first, they only register all these idiots who accept this measure voluntarily. All others, who refuse the 'chipping', will one day be forced to do it. But this will last several years.'

Alfred's eyes betrayed boundless anger. 'They mark us like pigs! I pray to God that I will fight until the day when this parasite scum pays for all its crimes! Never! Not me! Never ever!'

'I think that they plan to kill a large part of the population with these new Scanchips. Damn! I'm sure! Then the media will tell us it was a pandemic or something. The ideal way to solve the overpopulation problem,' lectured Frank.

'I gonna blast the skull of everyone who wants to register me with this shit!' shouted Alf, banging on the table.

In the following week, John Thorphy organized a few boxes of ammunition and several new guns in Moscow. Furthermore, Wilden had got new donations from some old friends whose names were still unknown. Frank, Alfred and about a dozen men from Ivas were on their way to Mazyr in the south of Belarus to join another demonstration.

After the protest march in Pastavy had ended in a bloody fiasco, Tschistokjow had changed his old 'rally-plan'. Now he wanted to 'jump' from one part of Belarus to the other to hinder the authorities to concentrate their police forces at one particular place.

Finally over 3000 people came to Mazyr and except for minor scuffles with the police, everything went quiet. This time the supporters of the freedom movement had huge banners with new slogans.

'Only Artur Tschistokjow can save us! Give him the power over Belarus!' or 'Artur Tschistokjow - Our last hope!' could be read on them.

In the meantime, the politician had recovered from the terror of the assassination attempt in Baranovichi, but he knew that something like that could happen anytime again. From now on, his guardsmen always checked the roofs of the houses around them before they held a rally.

The year 2034 ended, and when the first snowflakes came from the sky an unfamiliar calm returned. Wilden had organized a Christmas party which was this time held in the renovated church in the center of the village.
The majority of the villagers came and the building was finally bursting at the seams. Artur, whose family no longer existed, visited them and became very sentimental when he entered the church. For some hours, they all felt like ordinary people. A feeling that was meanwhile strange for Frank and his comrades. Wilden's moving Christmas speech, which had exceptionally nothing to do with politics, remained in Frank's mind for a long time.
Meanwhile, he was 33 years old. In the long hours of the dark winter evenings he mused a lot about his previous life, about what he had achieved - and what not.
'I'm some kind of hero - that's all!' he sometimes said to himself, not knowing whether he was really happy about this.
Concerning his personal goals in life, which included a woman he loved and perhaps even a family, he had achieved nothing so far. The fight against the global system, that seemed to become a never ending struggle, was eating up his life. It was slowly devouring it with each passing year.
Frank had to avow himself that he just marked time in all private things. He became aware of it all when he saw Julia and Viktor kissing and flirting at the New Year's party at the Wildens. Shortly after 24.00 pm, when several dozens of people had gathered in front of the

house of the village boss, he finally went back home, sad and frustrated. Alf still stayed for a few hours and came back early in the morning, totally drunk.

With the beginning of February the political struggle went on with full force. The governor of the sector 'Eastern Europe' announced the start of the registration of the population with the new Scanchips.

Meanwhile, the sub-sector 'Belarus-Baltic' had become a place of misery. The hard winter had claimed many victims among the homeless people in the cities across the country. Furthermore, the industry had further collapsed and a lot of production complexes had been outsourced to other countries. Hundreds of thousands had lost their jobs.

As ailing as the industry was also the power grid of the sub-sector. Power outages had become the new normality and especially in the cold months they had disastrous effects on the people.

Perhaps the year 2035 could be promising for the freedom movement and even make a revolt possible. Frank thought a lot about it, but he came to no solution. Only one thing seemed to be certain, Some of his comrades would not witness the next New Year's party.

'Well? What do you think about the leaflet?' asked Artur the village boss and looked expectantly at him.

'Hmmm...,' muttered Wilden and scratched his gray temples while he was translating the Russian text.

Now he was talking quietly to himself. Frank and Alfred sharpened their ears.

'People of Belarus, don't let them implant you a poison-chip!' was the headline of the leaflet.

Wilden studied the text thoughtfully and finally read out aloud, 'The new implanted Scanchip contains poison capsules! Defend yourselves against the criminals of the Medschenko regime and the World Government.'

'This is very good!' Wilden said with a smile.

'We have printed about 200000 of these pamphlets, our men distribute them everywhere in Belarus,' explained Tschistokjow.

For the 15th of February, he had planned another protest march. This time in Rechytsa, a small town in the southeast of the country, bordering the former Ukraine.

'This country has no more money. Have you already heard it? It was yesterday on television,' said the blond man.

'No more money?' returned Frank.

'Yes, the sub-sector 'Belarus-Baltic' is officially broken. How do you say it in German?' asked Tschistokjow.

'Bankrupt!' explained Alf.

'Okay! Bankrupt!' repeated the Belarusian and grinned.

'This is good for us. Then this sub-sector could probably fall into chaos this year. Great! I hope so!' said Wilden.

'I believe that, my friends. Soon, they will do not even have money to pay the policemen. No salary for the cops anymore! Do you understand?' remarked Tschistokjow.

'No more money for the clerks, the administrators, the police and so on?' marveled Frank.

'Yes, yes!' said Artur excitedly. 'There is only money left for this month. From next month on, they will be insolvent.'

Alf grinned. 'Well, then the cops will think twice before they risk their lives against us.'

'At least, the ordinary Belarusian cops. The GCF soldiers, however, are paid by the World Government itself,' added Frank.

'We must use the situation. Many people are still very poor and now the system in Belarus is crumbling even faster. Over 1,5 million Belarusians have no more jobs, no more money. Over 800000 people are homeless. It is like a boiler, the whole land is a boiler! Do you understand?'

'Belarus is fuming with rage,' spoke Frank and winked at Artur.

'It is fuming with rage everywhere! Yes!' shouted the Belarusian.

Apart from that, Artur thought that he had meanwhile reached a remarkable popularity among the people. The Belarusian dissident had almost become a prominent person, and was thereby also more vulnerable than ever before.

At the beginning of the year 2035, the freedom movement was no longer an underground organization, because it had grown far too much in the last time. Millions of Belarusians were sympathizing with the Rus, and among these people were no longer just the poor and disaffected.

Even more and more clerks and policemen secretly hoped for a change in their country. They had finally realized, that the policy of Medschenko was leading Belarus into chaos. Furthermore, the Rus had received larger sums of money from anonymous donors. Artur invested the money in building up a better organization, in propaganda material and in weapons, which were bought in Russia or in the Arab countries.

The power of the occupational regime in Minsk was wavering, and fortunately the World Government was paying only little attention to small and unimportant countries like Belarus or Lithuania.

The powerful men behind the global regime had other interests than caring for poor, tiny regions like the sector 'Belarus-Baltic' with its barely 14 million inhabitants.

Finally, the demonstration on February 15th was a great success. The local police remained passive and some of the officers even greeted the demonstrators friendly. Over 3000 members of the movement marched through the streets for three hours, almost looking like a civil war army.

Frank and Alfred were thrilled. Slowly but surely, the authorities of the sub-sector 'Belarus-Baltic' had more and more problems to suppress Tschistokjow's organization, especially in the small towns and rural areas. In some villages, the Rus already ruled the streets. Physicians, who worked for the World Government and implanted the new Scanchips, had been declared to 'enemies of the nation' by the Rus, and Tschistokjow's men threatened to kill them if they would not stop the registrations in Belarus.

Some of them were even shot by masked men in the open street after they had ignored the warnings of the rebels. Finally, the mass registration in Belarus stopped before it had really begun, because most physicians had no interest to risk their lives anymore. In the meantime, the men from Ivas were untiringly active, above all in the smaller towns. They distributed leaflets and stickers, hung up placards and supported the freedom movement as good as they could. In the rural regions, the conflicts with the police were meanwhile less frequent. Sven proudly told his comrades that he had given some leaflets to a group of policemen who had read them with great interest. The officers had just smiled at him and finally said that Tschistokjow was right.

Medschenko and his staff feared such things more than everything else, and police officers, who were caught ignoring the orders of their superiors, were immediately dismissed. Nevertheless, more and more ordinary Belarusian policemen had sympathies for the Rus.

'Look at this!' Frank's eyes became wide.

In front of him was a sea of people and flags. The men from Ivas had distributed thousands of leaflets in the last days, day and night, almost without any breaks. Moreover, Tschistokjow's radio stations and websites had supported the campaign for today's rally. And it had not been in vain.

More than 20000 people had come to the outskirts of Gomel and the crowd was still growing.

'It is unbelievable!' exclaimed Sven enthusiastically. 'What a giant mass of people! This is the biggest rally in the history of our movement!'

'Here we go again,' remarked Wilden, grinning from ear to ear.

Shortly thereafter, the crowd started to move. Slowly, accompanied by loud screaming and chanting. Step by step they marched towards the inner city. Who dared to stand in their way today would feel the power of an angry mass, ready for everything, as Frank thought.

'This is our first rally in a big city. I'm curious to see what's going on today,' said Alf with a faint tang of uncertainty.

'Don't worry,' returned Kohlhaas confidently. 'They don't want to mess with a crowd like that!'

The protesters unwaveringly marched towards the city center. Huge banners showed the numerous spectators of the rally slogans like 'Freedom is near!' or 'Work for all Belarusians!'.

More and more desperate men and women wanted to hear things like that, and Tschistokjow shunned no danger to carry his political claims also into the larger cities of the country.

Frank and Alfred hurried to the edge of the crowd and loaded their guns. Meanwhile, many of the Belarusian guardsmen knew their faces and treated them with respect and awe. After all, Frank had saved the life of their leader.

'Dawaj! Dawaj!' shouted Kohlhaas and signaled the armed troopers that they should follow him to the front ranks of the endless line of men and women.

The uniformed men obeyed. Shortly afterwards, the crowd reached a large square after they had passed a shopping zone full of rundown department stores. Here, the Rus encountered a great number of policemen.

'I greet you, my Belarusian brothers of the police! Please behave peacefully and we will do it too! You can listen to my speech and I hope that you will finally understand, that we want to liberate all our compatriots! Even our brothers who work as policemen!' shouted Tschistokjow into his megaphone.

'Shit! That's a damn big armada, and they don't look as if they just want to let us demonstrate here,' said Bäumer.

Three anti-riot tanks appeared from behind a wall, five more came out of a side street.

'This rally will last not longer than one hour! I only want to deliver my speech, and then we will leave Gomel immediately. In peace! I promise it!' said the leader of the Rus.

Now the policemen went in position behind some barricades and sandbags, then the just waited. A tall officer finally stepped forward, grabbed a bullhorn and gave Tschistokjow an answer, 'Everybody has to leave this place immediately! Cooperate or we shoot!'

'Hurry up! In position! Take your guns! Dawaj!' shouted Frank and waved the other guardsmen nearer.

The Belarusians took their rifles from their shoulders and hastily formed a firing line.

'I knew that something like this would happen. Gomel is no tiny village,' moaned Alf, staring at the police officer with the bullhorn.

Only a few hundred of the more than 20000 demonstrators were members of the militant section of Tschistokjow's organization. The biggest part of the crowd consisted of ordinary citizens; even women and children were among the people who had come the rally.

The guardsmen in their gray shirts tried their to bring women, children and old people to the rear part of the mass.

'I ask you to give us just one hour. Then we will leave the city immediately!' shouted Artur again.

'You won't get this hour from us, Mr. Tschistokjow! This rally will end now - or we will shoot your people down!' replied the officer.

'I'm sorry, but we will not go! I'll deliver my speech and you will have to shoot me to silence me! If you won't give us this single hour, many people will die today! On both sides! Please think about if it's really worth it!' threatened Artur.

A long minute passed and an uncanny whispering and murmur went through the large crowd which slowly became anxious. All guardsmen of the freedom movement had positioned themselves. Frank and Alfred were lying side by side on the asphalt. The police officer ran back behind his men and finally gave the order to fire. Some of the officers hesitated for a short moment, but then they started to shoot and the first protesters fell to the ground, screaming and bleeding.

'Fire!' screamed Artur after he had disappeared in the crowd.

A bloody firefight followed. Several dozen police officers were shot down by the Rus, while hundreds of demonstrators were mowed down by the hail of bullets which came from behind the barriers. Then even the anti-riot tanks joined the fight and returned fire with their Gatling machine guns.

Cries resounded from everywhere; bullets pierced through flesh and bones. Fountains of blood sprayed up in the crowd, while desperate outcries echoed in Frank's ears. A tall man, whose chest had been perforated by a direct hit, fell on his back. As a war-proven shooter Frank killed two police officers with precise head shots and sent three more of them to the ground Then he rolled the dead men to the side and jumped up.

'Come on, Alf! We can't win this fight!' he yelled, pulling Bäumer with him.

Meanwhile, the demonstrators were gripped by sheer terror and tried to escape through the side streets. Hundreds of dead and wounded people already covered the square. Finally, the tanks rolled forward and continued to fire at everyone in their way. It became a massacre.

'In that street there!' roared Alf and Frank followed him. A large swarm of people tried to break through a police barricade and the onrushing men and women ran directly into a deadly machine gun salvo. Then the first protesters attacked the policemen with iron bars, clubs or even bare fists. The armed guardsmen followed them and started to shoot while all hell broke loose.

Driven by boundless terror, the people beat down some policemen, who had blocked their way, and finally jumped behind the barrier.

'You damn rats!' screamed Frank and shot his entire magazine empty. Then he threw the rifle away and pulled a hatchet from his belt.

With a loud roar he smashed the head of a policeman in front of him, and tore his weapon out of the bloodspattered helmet of the man. Then he hacked down another and finally lost the hatchet, which was sticking deep in the shoulder of the screaming opponent. Meanwhile, the outnumbered officers retired from the side street. Many of them had already been shot or beaten to death by the raging crowd.

'They have tried to encircle us! Fuck!' shouted Alfred and picked up the pistol of a wounded policeman from the ground. He shot him in the chest.

The other people tried to escape through the now vacant street, dragging Frank and Alf with them. It was a giant chaos. The two men and a some Belarusians ran through an alley and attacked anyone who got in their way.

'We must get a car somewhere!' yelled Frank and turned into another street.

Some demonstrators followed them. Finally, they reached an intersection where a car was waiting in front of a stoplight. Frank immediately ran across the street, shot the side window to pieces and shouted something in Russian at the driver. A terrified man stared at him and did not dare to open his mouth.

'Get out of your car or I kill you!' hissed Frank and pulled the scared driver out of his car. He started the vehicle and sped off with screeching tires.

'Shit! Shit! Shit!' ranted Kohlhaas and raced like a madman through the streets.

'There! Highway! To Minsk!' Alf pointed at a rusty sign.

Some minutes later, they had left the inner city. When they saw Gomel becoming smaller in the background, they sent a short prayer to heaven.

'My nerves are still raw! Bloody hell!' gasped Bäumer, taking a deep breath.

'Those fucking cop bastards!' growled Frank, smashing his fist against the windshield.

The two men drove past Minsk, refueled and finally reached Ivas a few hours later. They had survived a terrible day.

Stubborn

The Belarusian police had shot down more than 2500 demonstrators. Hundreds more had been arrested. About 400 police officers had also been killed or wounded in the bloody firefight and during the following riots, that had lasted till the morning hours of the next day.

The media reported several days around the clock about the civil unrest and the street fights, mentioning the civilian casualties with no word. They told the people that Artur Tschistokjow had incited his followers to attack the police and turned around the facts in the usual way. The leader of the Rus was still shocked because he had never expected a bloodbath like this. But his first rally in a bigger Belarusian city had finally ended in a disaster, and there was no more room to put a gloss on it.

Furthermore, the Scanchips of all persons, who had been identified as protesters, had meanwhile been blocked. It meant that all these people lost their jobs and became homeless in the long term. After a while, they were not even able to buy a piece of bread anymore.

But these merciless terror measures had not the desired effect, because now still more people had nothing to lose anymore and looked up to Tschistokjow like to a savior.

Apart from that, more and more discontent spread among the Belarusian policemen, because of the fact that an increasing number of civil servants and officers got their salaries irregularly or had to accept wage cuts. Therefore, many policemen were no longer willing to risk their lives in bloody street fights or riots against

Tschistokjow's supporters. The leader of the Rus had meanwhile disappeared again after he had escaped from Gomel, accompanied by a group of heavily armed guardsmen. A little later, he tirelessly continued his struggle, driven by growing hatred and fanaticism. In his eyes, the massacre in the streets of Gomal had been another indication that the revolution would come in the near future.

Wilden and the other men from Ivas had escaped the chaos because they had decided to leave the city early enough. Nevertheless, two young men from the village had been killed by the police during the riots in the night.

Today, Artur Tschistokjow had come to Minsk where a few dozens of his lieutenants were waiting for him in a dingy restaurant in the south of the city. The demonstration in Gomel and its bloody consequences had paralyzed many of his followers, leaving them in a state of fear and insecurity.

One or two had already asked Artur to refrain public meetings and rallies in the future, but the rebel leader was fuming with rage inside and did not want to hear things like that.

Now he demanded perseverance from his followers. Tschistokjow walked to the end of the room, looked angrily around and started his speech.

'My dear comrades!
Bloody battles are lying behind us. Some of you have broken bones or even gun wounds. More than 2500 supporters of our freedom movement have soaked the streets of Gomel with their blood. The police has just

shot us down, just slaughtered men, women and children because they have claimed freedom!

But our eyes are still glowing with excitement, because now we stand closer together than ever before. The blood of the fallen soldiers is the glue which sticks us together. We have finally realized how determined our enemy is and now we have to show him that we are still a hundred, a thousand times more determined. We have to show them that we will sacrifice our lives without complaining. No guns and no tanks can stop us anymore. If we have to die for the survival of our nation, it is our duty.

We do not want to ask, what's good for us because our lives are unimportant. It is only important that our nation survives and our country will be freed from slavery! Like the old Rus, we want to be strong and don't want to fear death.

We will do the necessary things, endure all the pain with a smile and even die the martyr's death for the future of our children. If we have reached this state of inner freedom, then we can win the external freedom too!'

Tschistokjow's men were silent and just stared at him. The resentful speaker waved his forefinger and the burning gaze of his blue eyes touched the faces of his followers.

'If we march through the streets of another city, then our enemies will see that they haven't broken our spines. Then they will see our petrified glances and our iron will. And we will scream at them, 'Shoot! But don't think that you can stop the revolution anymore! Although you tear bloody gaps into our ranks, we will come back with even more comrades, again and again, and come back and bleed and bleed until your tyranny has fallen! I have seen many of my faithful comrades in Gomel, dying in the streets, and I have held their hands until their last breath. You all have it too! Now you must be strong, my brothers! Now, right now, you must be faithful, grim, hard, fearless, because now fate will prove us!

If we give up now and don't save our people, then our nation will be extinct. Then, all fighting has been futile and pointless. If we give up today, then all freedom fighters around the world can give up too because they also have to risk their lives and have to suffer and die for the new morning.

If we fail, the World Enemy will wipe out our nation in the next decades. Then all the sacrifices of our ancestors have been in vain. The nations of Western Europe are already close to their total destruction, and Russia is the only hope our mother Europe has in this dark age. If we fail, Europe with all its great nations will die a cruel and painful death.

And if Europe dies, the rest of the world will become a bleak desert. Then, the light will leave this planet forever - and will never return!

So this is the most important war which has ever been fought in mankind's history! Therefore, we have only to care about our fight, not about our little lives! We have no right to surrender in this battle, in front of our children and grandchildren and world history!'

Artur screamed it into the ears of his comrades and was shaken by anger and energy. Soon, his men felt moved as by an electric shock and the courage returned to their hearts again. Only a few doubters remained among them

141

after he had finished his preaching. The next rallies had already been planned, despite the carnage of Gomel. So Artur's followers finally took heart. What had these outcast and neglected men to lose anymore?

While the situation in Belarus escalated, also other parts of the world were shaken by discontent. Frank and Alfred saw it on television on 24.03.2035. There had been a rebellion on the Philippines. The regime of sub-governor Oquino was overthrown by a successful insurrection. Rebel leader Michael Arroyo had taken over the power, he had founded the former Philippine state again and had finally allied with Matsumoto's Japan.
Overnight, another fire had broken out in the Far East. Four years ago, when Japan had fought its struggle for liberation, there had already been some riots in many parts of the country. Now, the Philippine rebels, supported by Matsumoto, had actually managed it to break their chains and had conquered the city of Manila.
Frank and the others were beside themselves with joy. A second revolution had ended with a success and another state had resisted the power of the World Government. Within a few hours, all eyes focused on the Philippines and the international media were boiling mad.

'That's a true sensation!' shouted Wilden and jumped up and down in front of the TV.
Frank, Alfred and Sven clapped their hands. The latter tried it anyway because three fingers were missing on his left hand since the Japanese war. Nevertheless, also Sven's remaining eye lit up with confidence and hope.

'We can also do it!' said Frank smiling and raised his fist.

'Now the Philippines! This is another kick in the butt of the World Government!' cheered Alf.

'Matsumoto has his first official ally!' returned the village boss and looked triumphantly at the screen, where a reporter commented the pictures from Manila with a sardonic undertone.

Thousands of people were demonstrating in front of the presidential palace while Arroyo was delivering a speech.

'Let's see when the GCF will march in there!' remarked Alfred and stroke over his dark beard.

'They won't attack the Philippines. After all, the Japanese stand behind Michael Arroyo!' answered Wilden.

'Do you think that Artur has already heard the news?' asked Sven the others.

Frank looked at him and nodded. 'Well, I'm sure about that. It is on TV since hours.'

'It's going on in Asia! And it is time that we give the World Union another kick in the balls in Europe!' shouted Wilden.

Now the World President was interviewed. He appeared visibly confused and worried. The four men in Ivas laughed, however, uttering spiteful remarks.

In the course of the day Artur called them, completely beside himself with excitement. These great news from a distant part of the world had significantly increased his morale, and the Belarusian politician sounded more optimistic than ever. He told Wilden that he had planned a major offensive, full of publicity campaigns and protest marches for this year's summer. It was only a matter of time for him, until Belarus would fall into anarchy.

143

Apart from that, Tschistokjow had just a lot of luck because the World Government did not pay much attention to his movement, turning its view at more important regions of the world and leaving the fight against his organization to the regional authorities and Medschenko.

Frank, Alfred and the rest of the other young men from Ivas returned to Belarus in the following week to support the Rus in their tireless publicity campaigns for the freedom movement. For several nights they were even active in Minsk.

In early April, the Rus organized five concurrent demonstrations in small towns in the east of the country, each with about 1000 people. They were successful and except for some minor clashes with the police, they all ended without bigger problems. Sometimes the officers had simply looked away, leaving the demonstrators alone.

Today, Frank, Alfred, Artur and about hundred leaders of the guardsmen squads from all parts of Belarus had met on a large meadow, far out in the country. It was heavily raining, but Frank ignored the unpleasant weather.

'Frank and Alf, I will make you the leaders of my armed men. As I have already told you,' said Tschistokjow.

'Thanks!' answered Frank, feeling honored.

'Most of them can speak English. So you can talk to them,' explained the Belarusian. 'These men are the leaders of all my guardsmen units. I already told them that you will give them the orders from now on.'

Frank perked his eyebrows up. Then he grinned to himself. 'Am I some kind of general now?'

'Yes, exactly! You are the general of the guardsmen!'

'And Alf?'

Bäumer looked annoyed and felt ignored by Tschistokjow. 'Yes, what's about me?'

Artur mused for a minute. Finally he said, 'Frank will lead the northern units and Alf the southern units, okay?'

Alf shook his head. 'You can leave this honorable task to Frank. May he lead all these troopers. Meanwhile, I can watch his back.'

Frank laughed and winked at Bäumer. The blond Belarusian was musing again.

'Well, Alf, as you want it.'

'General Frank Kohlhaas!' said Artur, he clapped on Frank's arm.

'Your guardsmen need bulletproof vests!' meant Frank. He pointed at the troopers behind him.

'Ah, yes...' Artur was baffled for a second.

'Armor, helmets and so on,' added Frank with a grin.

'I see....' Artur was brooding and scratched his head.

'In Gomel, our men hadn't head any protection against bullets. But the cops had helmets and bulletproof vests.'

'Of course! You're right!'

Tschistokjow raised his hand and gazed pensively at the sky.

'Try to get this stuff, all kinds of armor, helmets and so on,' said Frank to Artur.

Shortly thereafter, he let the guardsmen muster and told them that they had to equip themselves from now on. Each trooper should get a helmet and any kind of body protection till the next rally. They spent the rest of the day with firing practices and Frank tried to teach the young Belarusians some basic military tactics. He loved his new role and enjoyed the respectful attention he received from his new 'soldiers'.

At the next demonstration in Luninyets, a bizarre sight was offered to the numerous inhabitants of the town, who were witnessing the spectacle. About 300 troopers had come with partly self-made armors. Some of them had strange looking vests of iron plates, others wore bulletproof vests which they had bought on the black market somewhere in Russia. Many guardsmen even had old helmets of the former Soviet army, the NPA and the German Wehrmacht.

Frank could not help grinning but the main thing was that the helmets, which were partly already many decades old, would protect the men.

'Better a weird looking helmet on the head than a bullet in the head!' said Frank to himself and grinned again.

And even the sparsely represented police reacted confused on the sight. Artur delivered a speech against the outsourcing of Belarusian factories to low-wage countries and earned thunderous applause from the people who were afraid of losing their jobs.

Otherwise, everything went smoothly and some police officers even greeted the 3000 demonstrators friendly. Artur was content.

One day later, Frank and Alfred drove back to Ivas. It was at the beginning of May. Meanwhile, Kohlhaas and Bäumer were 'on vacation', as they formulated it. They spent their time with hanging around in the living room or sitting in the kitchen, and made some walks in the woods, enjoying the first warm sun rays of the year 2035.

'Have you seen Julia in the last days?' asked Frank his friend.

They went deeper into the forest and finally sat down on a fallen trunk. Alf shrugged his shoulder.

'No, I haven't seen her. Perhaps she is in Grodno, with Viktor.'

'Yes, could be,' muttered Frank.

'I know, it annoys you...'

'Yes, could also be,' returned Kohlhaas sadly.

'Nevertheless, she likes you, Frank.'

'Pah! Of course! And why does she constantly visit that Belarusian?' hissed Frank angrily.

'You have told me that you have already...'

'Already what?'

'Well, you have...'

'Just forget about that!'

Alf looked at his friend in wonder. Then he said, 'You have kissed her. And then?'

'Yes, something like that. Well, not exactly, I mean...,' stammered Frank.

'Don't talk Chinese, Frank!'

'If she would be my girlfriend, she wouldn't be in fucking Grodno, okay?'

Alf just grinned and asked for details. 'Now, tell uncle Alf the whole, sad truth.'

'Fuck you!' ranted Frank, giving Bäumer a nudge with his elbow.

'Let's go!' he suggested and stood up from the trunk.

Alf could imagine that Frank had probably exaggerated a few months ago. The reality of his 'successful advance' towards the heart of Julia Wilden was apparently much more disillusioning than his euphoric 'reports of victory'.

'Nevertheless, we have kissed. Even though, it has been more amicable,' thought Frank and mirthlessly looked at the treetops which slowly became fresh and green again.

For a while they walked through the beautiful forest that surrounded the village. Both were silent. Perhaps the revolution, which they were all hoping for, was just an illusion, like Julia's love. Frank would still find it out soon enough.

Meanwhile, Wilden dealt less with his daughter and more with strategic preparations of political campaigns. Today, he had risen early in the morning and was sitting in front of his computer. The village boss was designing a new leaflet against the proposed 'approximation of energy costs' in the sub-sector 'Belarus-Baltic'.

This so called 'alignment' meant nothing else but a massive increase of prices for gas and petroleum which Medschneko's government had announced for October. Wilden had seen a report about this newest raid of the regime last night on television. The prices for oil and gas should be increased with not less than 60%, as the media had told the people. Perhaps this was another turning point in the lives of millions of Belarusians and could finally become the last straw that would break the camel's back.

While the country still had its own oil reserves, oil and gas were nevertheless imported from other regions. Moreover, the population of Belarus was suffering under the increasing prices for almost everything. This new 'approximation' finally shook the people to the core and made them angrier than ever before. Apart from that, the steady decay of the manufacturing industry and several tax hikes had driven countless Belarusians into a black hole of hopelessness and despair. Now the Medschenko regime tried to pull even more money out of their already empty pockets.

'Equalization of prices...,' whispered Wilden quietly to himself, staring angrily at the screen of his computer.

He went on to formulate the new leaflet and admired his meanwhile thorough knowledge of the Russian language. Then he looked thoughtfully out the window, typed on the keyboard again and suddenly startled up. Somebody had knocked on the door.

Frank tried to hurry up. Wilden's house was already behind the next street corner. The village boss had rung him up this morning and had excitedly explained that he had an important message for him.

Frank rushed past a row of empty houses and finally turned left. He was almost there. Some seconds later, he abruptly interrupted his run, gaped and gasped quietly. A police car was parking on the street and he could see Wilden who was talking to three officers. A few seconds later he went with them into the house. Frank jumped to the side and hid behind a wall.

'What the hell do these cops here?' it flashed through his mind. His heart started to pound like crazy, then he sprinted back home.

'Alf, Alf! Damn, where are you?' he yelled through the hallway.

Bäumer came down the stairs from the upper floor and slowly rubbed his eyes.

'What's up?'

'The cops! There is a police car in front of Wilden's house!' shouted Frank with a horrified expression.

'What?'

Alf was suddenly wide awake and almost fell backwards.

'The cops? What?'

'Yes, come with me and take your gun! Now!'

The two men ran down the street, reaching Wilden's house after a few minutes. Moments later, they hid in the yard of an vacant house behind a shed and waited. The police car was still there.

'This can't be true! There has never been a cop in Ivas! What does that mean?' whispered Frank softly, peering past the shed.

'I don't know,' muttered Alf nervously.

The two were silent, while Martin Brenner and his wife, Wilden's neighbors, came out of their house and stared at the police car which was blocking their gateway. What had happened?

'So the most of you are farmers, right?' asked the policeman with the globular face.

Wilden had both hands in his pockets and tried to evade the views of the officers as good as he could.

'Yes, this is a village of farmers,' he returned.

'No tej njemez? German?' said the other policeman.

'Yes, njemez. Tej hotshesh goworitch pa russkje?' answered Wilden with a smile and hoped that his offer to speak Russian would bring him some sympathies.

'Njet!' grunted the officer. 'We can speak English!'

Shortly afterwards, the policeman told Wilden that they had pursued some teenagers, who had sprayed an antigovernmental slogan on a wall - 'Down with the World Government!'

The mummed young man had vanished in the woods near Ivas. It had been some nights ago, as the officer explained.

'Did you see any suspicious persons here in this village?' he asked. Wilden tried to smile.

'No, I did not see three suspicious young men,' answered Wilden angrily, playing the indignant man. 'You have already asked me that...'

Suddenly one of the cops left the group and went into the kitchen, where Mrs. Wilden welcomed him with an anxious smile.

'Are you okay?' asked the man and grinned at her.

'Yes!' breathed Agatha Wilden silently.

Then the officer walked around and seemed to watch out for something, while Wilden tried to start a harmless small talk with his colleagues. He spoke about the many interesting sides of farming, the work in the village, seeding and harvesting and so on. Finally, he told the policemen that Lithuania was a very beautiful country full of nice people.

The two cops became a bit kindlier and accepted Wilden's offer to follow him into the kitchen to drink a cup of tea. For some minutes, the village boss seemed to calm down.

'Oh, you have many books!' it suddenly resounded out of the library in the next room and Wilden looked like he had been stabbed in the back. He stood up immediately, smiled at the officers and hurried into the library, where a cop stupidly googled at the countless books around him. Obviously, he could not understand the German book titles. Meanwhile, Agatha Wilden gave the two officers another delicious blackberry tea - and just smiled and smiled.

'Ha, ha! Yes, my hobby is history. Just a hobby. I like to read everything about history,' said Wilden, stroking nervously through his gray hair.

'Are these books legal?' inquired the officer with a harsh undertone.

'Yes, of course. These books are all for historical studies. For my little hobby. You know?'

'Nietzsche?'

The policeman stared at an old book and scratched the back of his head.

'Ha! Not very interesting. Just an old book,' laughed Wilden and shrugged his shoulders.

The officer put the book back on the shelf. Then he left the room. Wilden took a deep breath and wiped off some drops of sweat from his brow.

'I don't read at all. Reading is boring,' grumbled the officer and finally went back to the kitchen.

After the policemen had enjoyed their tea they left the house and shook Wilden's hand with a friendly smile.

'If I see any suspicious persons here in this village, I will call you immediately!' promised the village boss.

The officers nodded approvingly and the police car disappeared again.

The policemen had come to Wilden because the authorities knew him as the registered owner of dozens of houses in Ivas. Meanwhile, all the villagers had become more than upset, because this had been the first time when a police car had come to Ivas. Fortunately,

Wilden seemed not to had aroused the officer's suspicions and had mimed the upright and harmless taxpayer once more.

Shortly afterwards, they knew who had done the silly spraying in the neighboring village of Rajazov. It had been three still very young teenagers, whose families had moved to Ivas with Wilden's permission one year ago.

Frank, Alfred and Sven finally beat them up while the village boss threatened their parents to banish them, if something like this would ever happen again. But after a while, all had calmed down - even Frank and Alf who had reacted on the incident with a tantrum.

'What?' hissed Frank.

He opened the front door and looked at three hardly 16 to 18 year old guys whose heads were bandaged. Two of them had black eyes and a few scratches across their faces.

'What?' he yelled at them again. Now also Alf came to the door.

'We just wanted to apologize, Mr. Bäumer...and...uh...Mr. Kohlhaas,' said one of the teenagers quietly.

'Yes, all right! Accepted! The main thing is that you have understood that such stupid shit can lead to a giant disaster. Why have you done it so close to our home village?' growled Frank menacingly, standing in front of the frightened boys.

A 17 year old boy named Ingo Moser nodded and stammered, 'Yes, we are really sorry. We will never do it again!'

'This is healthier! Believe me!' hissed Alf and his eyes twinkled angrily. Meanwhile, Frank almost felt sorry for the beaten up boys. They had come to the doorstep like shy little dogs.

'We are sorry too. We didn't want to beat you so hard, but on the other hand you have deserved it. This stupid spraying has endangered the whole village,' said Frank who was cooling off slowly.

'What do you think the cops will do with us if they ever find out who we are?' added Alf.

'We just wanted to help the freedom movement. Sven always says...,' stuttered a chubby boy with red hair and freckles sheepishly.

'I'm gonna talk to him. Maybe Sven will allow you to join his group but you will follow his orders, okay? And here, in the proximity of our village, you will not spray or make any propaganda at all, otherwise I will eat you alive!' grumbled Frank and perked his dark eyebrows up.

'Yes...I mean...no...of course not, Mr. Kohlhaas,' wailed the chubby redhead.

'Tell your parents that we are sorry for the black eyes and so on. But this lesson is better than everything that awaits us, if the cops or even the GSA will ever show up here,' explained Frank and dismissed the teenagers.

'Thank you, Mr. Kohlhaas and Mr. Bäumer,' he could finally hear. Then the three boys walked off.

A few days later, Frank had arranged that the three teenagers could join Sven's group. When he went shopping in Steffen de Vries' little store and met the mother of the redhead, the woman only greeted him with a silent 'Hello!'. Frank did not care, if she was still offended, because the boys had deserved the beating, as he thought. In the following days, Wilden ordered increased security measures. HOK checked all the Scanchips of the villagers again and spent endless hours in front of his computer. He even revised the registrations of vehicles and planes once more.

Meanwhile, Julia had returned to Ivas. This time, Viktor was not with her. Frank just nodded silently when he saw her in the village. The young woman had immediately noticed that he was still angry and sometimes she tried to start a small talk with him, but Frank openly ignored her and was not willing to change his behavior.

Furthermore, Artur had planned another rally at the end of the month. This time he had chosen Lyepyel. The situation in the country had become even worse in the meantime. The economic and social decline had taken an alarming course, and now there were spontaneous outbursts of anger and indignation in many parts of Belarus.

In Pinsk, workers of a production complex had started a strike to enforce higher wages. In other cities it had been the same. The police had always to intervene and the strikes had ended with several dead and wounded people.

Medschenko's regime was under increasing pressure, while Tschistokjow's movement got a massive inflow of new supporters.

After a football match in Minsk there had been conflicts between young Belarusians and immigrants from Georgia and Kazakhstan, who were living in the north of the city.

The rival groups had attacked each other with baseball bats and knives and many people had ended in hospitals. Two Belarusians and one Kazak had been killed.

A few days after, some Belarusian youths had thrown a self-made bomb at a group of foreigners what had caused new riots which the police had quelled with sheer brutality. But the feuds between Belarusians and immigrants were not over. Four Kazaks were finally shot by an unknown man in front of a pub. Meanwhile, Minsk resembled a powder keg that was close to a giant explosion.

Growing Crisis

'Are you ready to die?' screamed Frank and waved a squad leader nearer. The man grinned cynically, while Kohlhaas gave him some instructions in Russian.

Shortly afterwards, the armed guardsmen flanked the demonstration at a distance of five meters. Meanwhile, most of the Belarusians respected Frank

After all, they had not forgotten that he had saved Artur's life. A huge crowd of people had gathered in the eastern part of Grodno, near an abandoned shopping street. Frank looked around and saw empty building and a lot of rubbish on the street in front of him.

This city was slowly dying, like the rest of Belarus. Hundreds of unemployed and homeless people came from everywhere, they welcomed the Rus with loud shouts.

Artur had allowed some of them to join today's rally if they behaved properly. But a few of them were already drunk and so the guardsmen had to send them back home, because Tschistokjow did not accept drunk people at a rally. Finally, over 30000 people had come to Grodno today, including many people from Gomel. Obviously, the massacre had not broken their will. To the contrary, now they had nothing to lose anymore and viewed Tschistokjow as their last hope.

Frank was curious what was awaiting him today. Julia had not come with him. For good reasons. If there would be bloody street fights like in Gomel, it was better for a young woman to stay at home. However, her heartthrob

Viktor was somewhere in the crowd. The handsome Belarusian had led the group of Grodno over a longer period, but a few months ago he had stepped back into the second rank and had left the leadership to another man. Perhaps this change of heart had something to do with Julia, as Frank thought.

He was still musing about this since the early morning hours, searching the crowd for his rival. Around noon, the protest march began. Hundreds of dragon head flags waved above the heads of the demonstrators. Half a kilometer away from their meeting place, the police and even some GCF soldiers were waiting for the Rus. So far, they were just observing everything.

At the top of the long human worm walked Artur beside some bodyguards with assault rifles in their hands. The Belarusian stared at the policemen with a black look and waited. Frank and Alfred finally came from behind, while Wilden stayed in the rear of the crowd. Meanwhile, the two German guardsmen had mummed themselves.

'It was better to watch these cops, who had come to Ivas, from the distance. At first, I wanted to go to Thorsten to ask him what they wanted, but this would have been the wrong decision,' said Frank.

'Maybe they already know our faces. I'm still worrying about this,' returned Alf.

Although the two men from Ivas had hidden their faces behind sunglasses and black scarfs, they had been a bit too careless at the other rallies in the last months. Any camera had already recorded their faces for sure, meant Bäumer. Today, both men wore old steel helmets which John Thorphy had bought for them somewhere in Russia. The helmets were some remainders of the former 'peace

158

troops' of the UN that had finally become the 'Global Control Force' after 2018. In addition, they wore bulletproof vests.

'Look at this!' said Frank with a grin, pointing at a hulking Belarusian trooper in front of him.

'This looks more than weird,' muttered Alf, because of the strange sight.

The Rus had a battered fireman's helmet on his head and a steel plate, attached on his chest. He looked like one of the rebellious peasants from the Middle Ages, who went to war with a makeshift armor to fight their evil landlord.

'I don't think that this will protect him from any bullets!' joked Frank and Alf giggled.

'Nevertheless, it shows some goodwill,' laughed Bäumer.

'Give all power to Tschistokjow! Down with Medschenko!' resounded a loud chorus out of thousands of throats through the streets.

The crowd was marching across a large square, surrounded by beautiful old buildings, and moved then towards a long main street.

On the sidewalks, many citizens applauded and yelled. Meanwhile, the most Belarusians seemed to like the freedom movement. Only a bunch of foreigners was screaming some insults in the background. However, the large crowd was an inspiring and impressive sight. The Rus finally reached another square in the middle of the city, right in front of the town hall of Grodno, the residence of the local administrator.

Artur started his speech and greeted his supporters and the countless citizens. Meanwhile, the police had gathered around the crowd, but was still outnumbered many times over. Shortly afterwards, even some anti-riot tanks appeared.

'If you believe, that we are already many people, then just wait and see how many we will soon be in Minsk, when the people of Belarus will finally rise against their oppressors!' shouted the blond man into the microphone. Thousands cheered. Frank could see that even some policemen smiled pleasantly. Artur continued in his usual manner, accusing the World Government and Medschenko to promote the decline of Belarus. His voice resounded across the square and he electrified the mass around him once again.

'There! Look!'

Frank pointed at the town hall where a man looked out a window on the upper floor.

'Look at him, my Belarusian brothers and sisters! Can you see him? This man at the window of this beautiful town hall? We all know this man! It is Jaron Kaminer, the administrator of this city, a minion in the service of the World Government! Yes, take a good, long look, Mr. Kaminer! Soon, we will send people like you packing!' yelled Tschistokjow.

The man disappeared behind the curtain and the angry crowd sent him a wave of insults and curses. Some troopers even pointed their guns at the window and shouted threats but Frank called them to order.

'I have the following request to the policemen, I promise by my honor that there will be no violence today, if you just let me speak!' proclaimed the rebel leader.

The officers did not react and remained as silent as before. Some of them nodded until their superior yelled at them angrily. Apparently, the policemen seemed not to be interested in another shootout. The police chief finally took a bullhorn and interrupted Tschistokjow. The crowd seethed.

'The next street fight starts in two minutes,' moaned Frank and took his gun from the shoulder.

The GCF soldiers, who were all no Belarusians, positioned themselves alongside the police and loaded their weapons. Frank gave some orders to the guardsmen who were also waiting for another firefight.

'This demonstration is illegal and all people have to leave this square immediately!' ordered the police chief.

'Let me speak for twenty minutes, then I will end this demonstration!' answered Artur.

'I have the orders to shoot at you, if you don't stop this rally, Mr. Tschistokjow!' shouted the officer. 'I don't want a second Gomel. My men have families too!'

'Well, I would like to speak for ten minutes, then we will leave this city - no riots, no violence. I promise it! I also want no second Gomel and I regret it very much that we had to fight against our Belarusian brothers from the police. Don't waste your lives for politicians who are nothing but traitors, leading this country into chaos. They don't care about your lives, you are their slaves, like everyone else. Do you really want to die for 500 Globes a month?' called Artur.

'Please wait, Mr. Tschistokjow!' replied the squad leader and consulted some of his colleagues.

Artur exhorted his followers to remain calm and peaceful, while Frank, Alfred and Peter Ulljewski rebuked some aggressive, young Rus.

It lasted ten tense minutes until the police chief took his bullhorn again and answered, 'All right, Mr. Tschistokjow! I give you ten minutes!'

'Thank you!' returned the leader of the Rus happily.

While Artur ended his speech in time, and finally gave the order for an orderly retreat towards the eastern part of Grodno, chaos broke out on the opposite side.

The police chief of Grodno and the leading officer of the GCF occupation troops started to argue loudly and Frank heard the men insulting each other in broken English.

Shortly afterwards, the Belarusian policemen just walked off the square, leaving the GCF soldiers alone. However, this was an outrageous scandal, and its ramifications should become clear in the following weeks. The march ended in peace. Only some young Belarusian hot spurs had tried to start a brawl but the guardsmen had immediately restored discipline.

'This is no adventure holiday for knuckleheads who want to make trouble. Those who can't behave, have to leave this demonstration. I have promised the police, that this day will end without another fight and you should thank me for this!' told Artur his supporters again and again on the way home.

'It has been an unbelievable success,' said Wilden.

The men, who were walking on this sunny day beside him across the village square of Ivas, agreed. However, only a few of them did really understand the full meaning of the incident in Grodno. But as always, the head of the village community was lecturing and tried describe the whole political situation, omitting no detail.

'Instead of a bloody street fight, the Belarusian police has cooperated with us,' remarked Frank.

'Now you exaggerate! Cooperated? Well, they just haven't been in the mood for murder and manslaughter again - as little as our men,' answered Alf.

'Anyway, some of the cops have shown sympathies for us,' remarked Sven.

Frank looked at Wilden. 'The system has avoided a confrontation, and finally lost a big part of its authority. The Belarusian policemen have violated their orders to safe their lives, in an important city like Grodno. This is, without any doubt, a huge success and shows that the freedom movement is meanwhile a political factor.'

'Frank is right! I have already discussed it with Artur. We will conquer the rural areas now, develop improved structures and recruit more guardsmen units in every village and every smaller town. They are no longer able to stop us,' said Wilden.

'What is the sense of this?' asked one of the young activists.

'The sense? Well, the great day! When the government in Minsk bites the dust,' told him Frank emphatically.

The group sat in Steffen de Vries' cafe which was almost overcrowded with so many guests. The chubby Belgian hastily came to their table and took some orders.

'Today, we are coffee house revolutionaries,' joked Wilden.

Some of the others looked at him with questioning glances and the village boss laughed and said, 'All right, folks! I'm just kidding!'

Then he rubbed his hands, grinned and drank a delicious milkshake - Steffen de Vries' specialty.

The media in the administration sector 'Eastern Europe' almost hushed up the demonstration in Grodno. In some news reports the protest march was only mentioned with a few words. On television, they spoke of 'several hundred anarchists and extremists' and simply ignored all other facts. Meanwhile, heads started to roll at the Grodno police department. The squad leader and his entire staff had already been removed for disobeying an direct order from the government and the Scanchips of some policemen had been blocked for an indefinite time.

Now, many of the despaired officers were openly complaining about the situation in Belarus, what triggered even more drastic measures against them. The GSA, which had paid little attention to Belarus so far, sent now a small unit to Minsk to analyze and monitor the behavior of the local police. But all in all, the World Government did not expect a serious revolt in Belarus, a country with a population of hardly a dozen millions. No further GCF units were sent to Belarus because they were needed much more urgent elsewhere. The GSA was more concerned about Russia and the Ukraine where poverty and discontent were spreading like a plague.

While rebellious underground groups played no significant roles in Russia and were furthermore hopelessly fragmented, Artur Tschistokjow had formed a small but powerful movement under his leadership. Nevertheless, the GSA did not take him very serious - and this was his luck.

It was a warm evening and a mild wisp of wind was blowing across the meadow in front of Sven Weber's house. Frank and Alfred had returned to Ivas a few days ago after they had met with Artur and other members of his organization in Slonim.

While the Belarusian politician let no day pass without expanding his freedom movement, Frank and Alfred had decided to enjoy some free days in their home village. This evening, they had gone to Sven to sit with him and his parents in the garden to drink a cold beer.

'Artur is planning a nationwide strike in Belarus and Lithuania in the middle of October. If his plan is successful, we'll have good chances,' said Frank.

Sven's remaining eye looked at him annoyed, and the expression of his disfigured face showed that he did not want to talk about politics today.

'What's up?' asked Frank.

'Let's choose another topic,' suggested Alf.

Frank put him off. 'Okay!'

'Yes, Artur may do whatever he likes. Another beer?' said Sven, reaching into a small cold box on the ground.

With a faint clicking sound he pulled a beer out of it. Alf's eyes gleamed. 'Good idea, bring it on.'

'What is Julia doing right now?' muttered Frank. Mrs. Weber grinned and winked at him.

'Now, it's Julia time!' moaned Bäumer, rolling his eyes.

'Alf also needs a woman, what do you think?' said Frank to the others and clapped his friend on the shoulder.

'You should find a girl at first, buddy! And if you still have another woman left, you can give her to me,' replied Alf.

'Mr. Bäumer!' said Mrs. Weber with a chuckle.

'Leave me alone with that women thing!' hissed Sven.

At this moment, he became aware of the fact that every woman would try to run away when she saw him. The Japanese war had reversed the former undoubtedly attractive face of the young man with a maimed grimace.

'My boy, you'll also find a nice woman one day. Every Jack has his Jill,' remarked Mrs. Weber and patted her son.

'I know what you mean. My Jill would look like Frankenstein's bride,' answered the young man with a cynical smile.

Sven's father avoided any comments and his son seemed to be happy about it. Frank tried to turn the conversation to another topic.

'Have you seen these young boys again? I mean those who have done that spraying in our neighboring village?'

'They have been with us in Grodno,' said Sven. 'They are all right now, and very active.'

'Right, we must care for our young activists,' remarked Alf and grabbed the next bottle of beer.

'But they're still a bit scared of you,' answered Sven.

'Damn, we were really pissed off on that day, because of the cops and...,' said Frank.

'Anyhow, they have deserved the punishment. I have already talked turkey with them. Meanwhile, I can't say anymore bad things about them. To the contrary, they are good activists now.'

It was getting dark. Sven brought some candles out of the house and put them on the plastic table in their midst, his parents had already gone to bed.

Suddenly they heard steps. The outlines of a slender person, coming nearer, could be seen from afar. It was Julia Wilden.

'Ah, here you are! I've been looking for you everywhere. What are you doing?' asked Wilden's daughter and smiled. 'Can't you see it? We're boozing!' said Frank gruffly and emptied his bottle with a single sip.

'What's up?' Sven looked up.

'Nothing! I just tried to say hello!' replied Julia.

Frank distorted his mouth and looked at the pretty blonde.

'You have been a rare guest in the last time.'

'I know, but today I just wanted to stop by.'

Alf shrugged his shoulders, while Frank smiled sardonically.

'Your father has told me that you have once again been in Grodno. With Viktor, the great rebel.'

'Thus, I'm back now,' she answered quietly.

'Do you want to drink a beer?' asked Sven and held up a bottle.

'No, thank you! I sit down, okay?'

'But it is nice that you delight us with your presence, madam,' quipped Frank, grinning ironically.

Julia was silent and looked down at the plastic table. Kohlhaas was irritated.

'What's about your pretty Viktor? Is he still active in the movement? Now, tell something!'

'I don't know,' she whispered afflicted.

'You don't know, Julia? Is your Viktor still a member of the movement - yes or no? Or has he meanwhile started a career as male model?' sneered Frank.

'I do not know. He in the Grodno and I'm here,' she said and looked away.

'We already know that, Julia. Anyway, we can only see you, while Viktor seems not to be here. So what has

167

happened to Mr. Pretty?' teased Frank and grinned at her contemptuously. Sven was confused.

'All right, then I'll go now,' said Julia, stood up and walked away.

Frank drank another beer and was somehow irritated. Eventually, he went home and fell asleep immediately. Julia no longer interested him. At least, he tried to believe this.

Artur Tschistokjow sent some of his best men to Russia and the Ukraine to get in touch with other underground groups of dissidents in order to form an alliance.

Peter Ulljewski traveled to Moscow and met some members of the 'New Flag', a group of patriotic Russians who wanted to have their old country back.

Other proponents of the 'Freedom Movement of the Rus' went to St. Petersburg, Kiev, Volgograd, Novgorod, Ryazan, Rostov, Tula and about two dozen other cities. Here they met other rebels of various kinds. In the most cases the talks were successful and an initial cooperation could be organized.

Tschistokjow had meanwhile realized that Belarus would be nothing but a base for a far greater revolution in Russia and in the Ukraine in the long term.

Therefore, it was necessary to find more allies beyond the borders of Belarus. The hotbed, made of poverty, fear and ethnic tensions, was very fruitful in Russia. However, it lacked the numerous small groups of leadership. None of the other rebel groups in Russia had achieved much so far. Often it were only small and insignificant bunches of malcontents. Nevertheless, the TV reports about Tschistokjow and his movement had also impressed the political dissidents in Russia and the Ukraine. They admired the young politician and saw it as a great honor, if one of his representatives visited them. Wilden had also a high goal. He resumed contact with his old friend Masaru Taishi from Tokyo and asked him to organize a meeting with a member of the Japanese government. The village boss hoped that Matsumoto's state would financially support them.

Finally, Mr. Taishi managed it to arrange a meeting. The Japanese businessman became not tired to emphasize that his friend from Lithuania had sent the Japanese army two 'heroes of Okinawa'.

Foreign minister Mori himself eventually gave Wilden the chance for a short talk. A few days later, the village boss flew to Japan.

Frank was meanwhile sure that Julia and Viktor were no longer together.

'He has just exploited me!' complained the beautiful woman and tried to find solace at Frank. But Kohlhaas cold-shouldered her and pretended to have no time for 'women's stuff' - after all, the revolution was calling for him.

Nevertheless, the fact that his secret love seemed to be interested in him again was inspiring. In the following weeks, the freedom movement made two more rallies in smaller towns and got a lot of support from the locals. The few policemen, who watched the demonstration, behaved passively or even cooperatively, avoiding any confrontations.

Artur finally managed it to meet the chief of the local police for a brief talk after the demonstration.

Meanwhile, Wilden was in Japan since two days. Frank racked his brain about what he would achieve by talking with the Japanese foreign minister. His friend Alf was curious too. However, both had the greatest ideas and sometimes literally fell into daydreams.

But the former businessman from Westphalia did not disappoint them. He proved himself, in the conversation with Akira Mori, the closest friend of president Matsumoto, as a brilliant diplomat and negotiator. He managed to convince the foreign minister of Japan that the freedom movement actually had a realistic chance to take over the power in Belarus.

Apart from that, Japan urgently needed more allies and partners who supported them in their fight against the World Government. After the Philippines had won their independence, under Japanese protection, and the GCF was not risking a further war in the Far East, it sounded more than tempting for Mori that there could really be a successful revolution in an European country.

Finally, the foreign minister of Japan promised Wilden some bigger deliveries of arms and moreover financial support.

A few days later, Tschistokjow got a donation of not less than fifty million yen from the Japanese state what changed the situation abruptly. Inspired by his success, Wilden returned to Belarus and told Artur the great news. Artur could hardly believe what he heard and was beside himself with joy. Now the political success had to follow.

It was pleasantly warm in this beautiful summer night. Frank, Alfred, Sven and about thirty Belarusians had made their way to Klaipeda and were waiting for a merchant ship. They were tiredly hiding in the darkness behind a huge wall of metal containers at the port.

'What's the time?' asked Sven.

Frank held his watch under the light of a street lamp.

'Quarter past two!' he muttered.

'I hope that they really come,' grumbled Alf and lit a cigarette.

'The Japs have said between two and three o'clock,' answered Kohlhaas and yawned.

One of the Belarusians bugged him shortly thereafter with the same question, in barely understandable English. Frank reacted angrily and chased him away.

After half an hour, a merchant ship appeared at the docks. 'Brazil' could be read on the bow of it.

'It must be them!' whispered Frank and waved the others nearer.

Shortly afterwards, the ship docked at the port and the rebels crept forward. Nobody could be seen anywhere because the loading port of Klaipeda was a lonely place in the middle of the night.

'Konban wa!' shouted a man out of a hatch of the ship. Then he opened a large access door.

'Hello!' said Frank, and went with the rest of the men on board.

They shook the hands of the Asians and went below deck. Here was a huge room full of banana crates, about a hundred or even more, as Frank guessed.

'Watashi wa captain desu!' said a smiling Japanese.

'He is the captain of this rusty ship,' translated Frank with a grin.

The Japanese opened one of the boxes. 'Look! Very good guns from the army of Japan!'

'Where are the bazookas?' asked Kohlhaas.

The man opened another box and Frank took a look at some modern anti-tank weapons. He clapped the Japanese on the shoulder.

Then he nodded at Alf. Frank and the others brought the banana crates to several trucks and disappeared as fast as they could. The Japanese had kept their promise and further deliveries of arms from the Far East followed.

The weapons were hidden at various secret places in northern Belarus. It was a big arsenal: assault rifles of all types, hand guns, bazookas and even portable rocket launchers with automated target acquisitions to fight Skydragons or bombers. The men of the freedom movement were quite amazed. It was a blessing that the Japanese foreign minister had not denied their wishes and apparently believed in the success of their struggle.

Medschenko under Pressure

'What was the name of that dump again?' shouted Frank from the back seat.

'Legatzk! I have already said it many times,' answered John Throphy annoyed.

'How far is it?' asked Wilden.

'Maybe three miles,' muttered the Irishman and accelerated the car.

'Why hasn't Artur invited me to the meeting? I will ask him!' murmured Alf with a questioning glance.

'I don't know. He will probably have a reason,' meant the village boss and fumbled on the collar of his trench coat.

The car jolted over an old cobbled street and turned left. Finally they reached a rundown village. Except for an old woman, who was slowly walking across a muddy road in front of them, they did not see anybody.

After about three hundred meters the car stopped and a man in a gray shirt waved at them from a side street. They had reached their goal.

Wilden got out first and looked around. Dilapidated houses, some vacant, were on both sides. The men from Ivas followed the Belarusian.

'Come in!' said the guardsman, greeting briefly and leading them into a house.

Everything here seemed to crumble and the building looked like a ruin. Then they went up some stairs and finally entered a large room. About twenty men were waiting here, and Artur hurried to meet them.

'I greet you, my friends,' he said with a smile and shook their hands.

The men in front of them sat at a long wooden table and Artur made some remarks in Russian. Frank could not understand everything because the blond man was talking very fast. Shortly afterwards, he came back to his German friends and the Irishman.

'We are talking today about the new government of Belarus, after the revolution,' he said gravely.

'A new government?' asked Frank with surprise.

'Yes, if we reach our goals, we will need a new government in this country.'

'Aha?' Wilden wondered.

'Is this the reason for the meeting?' asked Alf with wide eyes.

'Yes, right!' answered Artur. 'I want Mr. Wilden and Frank in my government.'

'Well, I understand,' returned Alf a bit offended. He took a glass of mineral water.

Tschistokjow told his Belarusian comrades again what Wilden had achieved for the freedom movement with his journey to Japan. The village boss earned admiring looks, some of the men even applauded.

They knew Frank as well. He had saved Artur's life and was meanwhile the commander of the most important trooper squads of the organization.

The leader of the Rus looked at Wilden and said, 'I want you to be the 'foreign minister' of Belarus.'

'Foreign minister?' said Frank, raising his eyebrows up.

'Yes, the foreign minister of Belarus,' stressed Artur. Wilden smiled and thanked Artur for the honorable offer.

'Frank, you will be the commander of the army of Belarus. Do you agree?'

Kohlhaas was initially confused and paused. He briefly looked around and nodded then thoughtfully.

'All right!' he returned and smiled at Artur.

'Well, I'm happy. You are good fighters,' said the Belarusian and seemed to be pleased.

'And these are the other members of your cabinet?' asked Wilden, looking at the men at the table.

'Right! This is Dr. Gugin. Previously he has been at the university in Minsk. He was a lecturer. Dr. Gugin will be the minister of economy.'

An elderly man with a shrunken face, a bald head and bright gray eyes rose from his seat and shook their hands.

'Peter Ulljewski will be the commander of the new secret service,' explained Artur, pointing at his oldest friend.

Frank gave the sturdy street fighter a wink and grinned.

'A good idea!' meant Wilden.

'Mr. Juri Litschenko from Vitebsk, he will be the minister of the interior. Mr. Gregori Lossov will be the minister of defense...'

Two middle-aged men stood up and bowed. Now Tschistokjow introduced also the rest of the men to his German friends. They all would play a major role in the new, revolutionary Belarus, as the leader of the Rus planned.

'Well, congratulations!' Frank heard from the side. It was Alf.

Bäumer seemed to feel like a fifth wheel in this illustrious round of revolutionaries and Frank felt visibly uncomfortable. Nevertheless, he was proud that Artur had made an offer like this to him.

'If there will ever be a revolution, then I'll give you an important position,' appeased Frank his best friend.

'Yes, yes, do what you want, great master!,' grumbled Alf and turned round.

'Shall I ask Artur?'

Alf interrupted Frank rudely. 'No! Forget it!'

After an hour they left the Belarusians and drove back to Ivas.

Frank was thinking about the future, while Alf was staring out the window, and Wilden lectured about his first measures as 'theoretical foreign minister' of the new Belarus.

Kohlhaas could feel the boundless enthusiasm of the village boss because of Artur Tschistokjow's plans. But he was still skeptical concerning all these revolutionary dreams. Maybe it would be nothing but a figment in the end.

The Rus spent the sunny July of 2035 with ceaseless agitation. They made three smaller demonstrations in the west of the country. It came to no significant conflicts with the local police and Frank grew more and more into his role as a trooper leader.

Meanwhile, tens of thousands of pamphlets were flooding the land, and virtually the entire village youth of Ivas and thousands of Belarusians were active in Belarus and Lithuania day and night. Tschistkjow had preached his men that the revolution had to come in this year. A growing number of people was showing open sympathies for the Rus, while the state authority was crumbling more and more in many regions of the country. Often the policemen just looked away, left the streets to

Tschistokjow's men and let them distribute their propaganda. This was already a huge success.

At the same time, the situation in Belarus got worse. In August, the food prices climbed upward again and there were strikes and riots in the bigger cities. Furthermore, the feared increase of the prices for oil and gas was still coming. It was planned for October.
During the cold winter months, this hated new measure could finally cause a revolutionary mood. However, Artur and Wilden believed this, and the rapid growth of the movement seemed to prove them right. Once, their organization had been nothing but a small group of discontent people, but now thousands of Belarusians were coming to the dragon head banners. In August, the Rus finally planned to return to Gomel.

It was a beautiful autumn day. The bright rays of the sun were caressing the city of Gomel, the city which had seen a bloody massacre no Rus would ever forget.
Frank, Alf and Artur could not believe their eyes. They stood in the midst of a giant sea of people. Artur told them that today almost twice as many people as at the last demonstration had gathered in the city center.
'This is incredible. What a crowd! I think between 30000 and 40000 people,' marveled Frank.
'Hardship is driving them to us,' said Wilden soberly, eyeing the crowd.
'If they don't shoot us down again today, the Medschenko regime will lose its face,' meant Frank and stared at some policemen in the distance.

'Come on!' said Alf and pulled his friend on the sleeve of his gray shirt.

Then they went to the uniformed guardsmen. Frank gave them some orders and the men walked off. He turned to Bäumer and remarked, 'Today we have more than 3000 armed troopers here. This time, the cops will get a very bloody feedback if they attack us again. A few hundred guardsmen are waiting in the side streets, in smaller groups. Now we can encircle them too. But I hope it won't end in another bloodbath.'

'Good idea! I hope the same. Meanwhile, both sides have become more cautious and I can't imagine that the cops will risk another shootout,' speculated Alf.

Shortly afterwards, the mass started to move and headed towards the town hall of the city. Defiant chants resounded through the crowded streets and hundreds of flags were waved.

Today they were more than just a mass of discontented demonstrators. This was a small army that could meanwhile withstand the police forces. All the officers, who were stationed in the east of Belarus, had been sent to Gomel by the Medschenko regime. It showed the importance of this second rally.

The protesters marched about five miles through downtown and finally reached a large square. Here was the town hall. Artur delivered a speech which lasted almost two hours and shouted out his usual accusations against the government in Minsk, while he promised the people of Belarus a better future under his leadership. The policemen behaved restrained.

'They do nothing. Despite their anti-riot tanks and the other stuff!'

Frank was surprised and pushed up his steel helmet a bit. 'Maybe it will end peacefully today. The cops will also think twice before they start to shoot at us again,' said Alf.

After a while, a police officer came towards them and made his way through the crowd. Many demonstrators yelled insults at him. Nevertheless, the man walked straight to Artur and started to talk to him.

'What's happening?' asked Frank and looked in the direction of Alf.

Bäumer came to him. They pushed some men to the side and could finally see something. The two friends from Ivas paused and did not trust their eyes anymore. The policeman shook Artur Tschistokjow's hand, smiled and went back to his men.

Then the leader of the Rus shouted something into his megaphone.

'What has he said?' asked Alf.

'Artur has given the command to march off. The demonstration is over,' translated Frank.

'What do you mean?'

'We're going home! Closing time for today.'

'Huh?' Alf was puzzled.

'No shooting, no killing, just going home, Bäumer.'

The huge crowd peacefully left the inner city with amazing discipline. Some police units followed them and almost looked like companions this time. Eventually, the crowd dissolved and the protesters went home. Except for some quarrelsome young people, who started a few brawls on the way home, everything went smoothly. Finally, Artur departed with a satisfied smile at the end of the day. The second protest march through Gomel had been a triumph.

'Why haven't the GCF soldiers done anything?' wondered Alf and fetched something to drink.

'Simply because they have been far too few. The Belarusian police has denied to support them anymore. Alone they wouldn't have had a chance against 3000 armed guardsmen,' said Wilden.

'On television they have almost hushed up the rally in Gomel,' replied Frank and sat on the old office chair in Wilden's study like a king.

'About what shall they report this time? About the fact that they can't stop us anymore? That they have already lost a part of their power? Ha, ha!' laughed the village boss, slapping his thighs.

'You're right!' said Frank.

The former entrepreneur stood up in front of him and Alfred. 'This has been our greatest victory ever! The system has capitulated in Gomel. Do you really understand this?'

'Well, I think you're right, Thorsten,' answered Alf. 'Maybe they have really drawn in their horns in front of such a great mass of people.'

'The most important thing is that the Belarusian police has ignored Medschenko's orders. I agree with Artur in that point,' added Frank.

This time, the village boss had assessed the situation perfectly correct. The mass demonstration in Gomel had been an unexpected success. While the last rally had ended in a bloodbath, the second demonstration had ended without bigger problems and with twice as many people. Frank, Alf and Wilden discussed and drank until late at night. They implored the success of their revolutionary efforts and gave each other hope and confidence.

Eventually, Frank and Alf walked back home, totally drunk, loudly singing the hymn of the Rus. They fell blustering into the hallway of their house and crawled babbling on their beds.

'We...will...make it somehow...,' muttered Kohlhaas, while Alf let out a thunderous burp. A moment after they fell asleep.

In the darkness of the night Frank had a strange dream. In his mind's eye he could see the picture of a giant spaceship. Its body of steel was only weakly illuminated by some stars in the distance, and it was gliding silently through the endless black void.

Suddenly, Frank could see the interior of the spacecraft. Hundreds of people were huddling there. It were soldiers, wearing futuristic looking suits of armor of a metallic material. The faces of the men were full of fear. Some of them had closed their eyes and seemed to pray, others just looked nervously around, as if something terrible would wait for them. A tall man with a bionic arm, a scarry face and short hair came to the men and said, 'Try to calm down! In one hour we will reach the orbit of Ryann III. Then our journey is over.'

The soldiers were silent, looking anxiously at him. The tall man, apparently the leader of the unit, remarked, 'I see it in your eyes. You are afraid of the things which may encounter us on Ryann III. I know, the Rachnids are terrible enemies, but they are not invincible. We must defend the capital of the planet at all costs. There is no other way!'

'Is it true that the Rachnids have creatures which are bigger than an imperial tank?' asked a young man with trembling voice.

'Yes, my boy. But even these creatures can be killed!'

The man slapped on the young soldier's back with his metallic hand and the blond boy nodded.

After a while, the spaceship reached the orbit of the planet whose atmosphere was threateningly glowing in a reddish light. The men went into their drop pods and were ejected from the star ship. They cut through the blazing red sky like hailstones, and finally hit the planet's surface.

A steel door opened with a loud rumble and the frightened soldiers stormed across a desert plain. They had landed in the middle of a battlefield. Around them countless dead soldiers, tank wrecks and alien creatures covered the dusty ground.

The outlines of a vast horde of insect-like creatures were looming on the horizon. Between the smaller aliens, giant monsters with scythe-like claws were stamping forward, uttering fearsome screams.

'They are legion! How shall we defend this city against an entire swarm of Rachnids?' moaned a soldier, clutching to his laser gun full of worry and fear.

'We will hold the line, together with our comrades from Ryann III. It would be a disaster, if these aliens would ever conquer this planet. This is the junction of the whole space sector,' answered the troop leader with a severe look.

The soldiers were waiting while the veteran was staring at them. Horror and fright marked the often youthful faces of his men, and it became worse with each passing second.

Meanwhile, the fearsome enemies were slowly coming nearer. It were thousands of creatures. Hissing monsters with spiky, gleaming teeth and razor-sharp claws.

'You can always win, if you have a brave heart! Remember our ancestors, soldiers! Remember Artur the Great and Farancu the Brave!' shouted the veteran and his men regarded him in silence.

'But Artur the Great and Farancu and the Birth-War...these are all just ancient legends', replied the blond boy with a cynical smile.

The troop leader walked towards him and looked deep in his eyes.

'My boy, I am sure that every legend has a true core. Artur the Great has fought against a much greater number of enemies - many millennia ago. His foes were countless, it is said, like the stars of the galaxy. But he saved the light-born people from extinction, in a dark age without hope. Only his strong will and his courageous heart gave him the strength to fight on, even in hours of deepest despair. And it was the same with his general Farancu the Brave, who always fought against a superior enemy.'

'But I'm not Artur the Great or Farancu the Brave, I'm just an ordinary man,' answered the young soldier.

'You can become like them, my boy! You all can become like them! If Artur the Great would not have had the courage of a lion, fighting with contempt for death, there would not exist an empire of mankind today.'

183

A loud roar from an alien beast in the distance interrupted the speech of the troop leader. He smiled grimly, then he screamed at the top of his lungs, 'Remember him, remember the Holy Kistokov, the savior of the light-born people, the forefather of the Aureanic caste, the Redeemer of the righteous!

His successors led us Aureans to the stars but without him all light on earth would have been extinct long ago. The Holy Kistokov has defeated hardship, fear and despair! And we can also defeat these monsters! Be fearless and follow me!'

'Why hasn't Artur the Great just brought peace?' asked the young soldier the veteran.

'Peace? In the grim darkness of this present there is only war. Peace is nothing but an illusion,' answered the squad leader and activated his laser gun as the snarling horde of alien monstrosities started to rush forward.

Frank startled up like stung by a tarantula. He jumped out of his bed and looked confusedly around. The strange vision had almost left his head again and only his shabby, dark bedroom was still there.

'General Farancu! Farancu the Brave...' he muttered quietly to himself. 'What a nonsense.'

Frank hid his head under the blanket and tried to sleep, but weird thoughts disturbed him for hours and he found no more rest in this night.

Vitali Medschenko, the governor of the sub-sector 'Belarus-Baltic', looked out the window of his splendidly equipped office. His eyes wandered across the busy main street which was close to the government district of

Minsk. Meanwhile, he was waiting for his guest since two hours. In a corner, an old, gilded clock was ticking loudly and the penetrating noise interrupted the thoughts of the politician again and again.

Eventually, he put the clock in a drawer where he could not hear the annoying ticking anymore. Outside the government building a black limousine appeared in the same moment and a well-dressed chauffeur opened a door to let out a middle aged man with dark, curly hair. The visitor had arrived.

Medschenko scratched his broad forehead and stared with his bulging brown eyes at the office door. Then he heard footsteps in the hall, they became louder - the guest entered the room.

'Mr. Medschenko, I apologize for the delay,' said the man informally and sat down with a cold smile.

'Yes, no problem, Mr. Chernin,' answered the governor.

'How's your wife?' asked the visitor.

'Well, we have been in Rome three weeks ago. It's really nice there. My son and my three daughters have also joined our trip,' told Medschenko and offered a juice to his guest.

'No, thank you!' replied Chernin and looked away.

'Have you been at the lodge meeting in Moscow?' asked the chubby governor grinning.

'Yes, of course...' said his guest soberly.

'What can I do for you, Mr. Chernin?'

The black-haired man smiled sardonically. 'Well, can't you imagine, Mr. Medschenko? We demand an explanation concerning some incidents in your sector,' returned Chernin and put on a frown.

'You mean the demonstrations of this crazy troublemaker Tschistokjow?'

'Yes, what else? We have heard that this agitator can lead thousands of people through the cities of Belarus.'

'Well, that's not true, Mr. Chernin.'

The guest folded his hands and interrupted the governor harshly, 'No, it is true, Mr. Medschenko! Our GSA agents have told me about Gomel. About 30000 of these so called 'freedom fighters' have marched through the streets and the security forces haven't done anything.'

Medschenko swallowed. 'The behavior of the local police was not correct. But this was an unique occurrence. Such an incident will never happen again.'

'An onetime thing, right?' Chernin gave the politician a piercing look.

'Yes, there is no reason for any panic!'

'No reason? That's an odd thing. I have heard several GSA reports about incidents like that! How can you explain this, Mr. Medschenko?' hissed the guest.

'The police in Gomel had just not been prepared well enough last time,' answered the governor, clutching at the arm of his chair.

'Not well prepared? Is it true that the police chief of Gomel has not supported our GCF units, that he has violated the order to fire, and that he has furthermore shaken the hand of Tschistokjow? Is it true that he has made arbitrarily agreements with these Rus, following the motto, 'If you behave peacefully, then we do it too?' Give me an answer that convinces me, Mr. Medschenko. I haven't come all the way from Moscow to Minsk to listen to silly excuses.'

186

'Thus, it is not easy to smash this freedom movement overnight with our means. We need more support. Moreover, our coffers are empty,' explained Medschenko.

Chernin immediately stood up and pointed his forefinger at the governor like the lance of a tournament's knight. For several seconds he fixed the corpulent politician with his dark eyes. Medschenko was holding his breath.

'The GCF forces around the world have much more important things to do than worrying about regions like Belarus. I leave it to you to stop Tschistokjow by all available means. Clean up in the ranks of the police and put down this Rus scum. Arrest and liquidate anyone who professes himself publicly to this ridiculous 'Freedom Movement of the Rus'.

You have enough resources, if you just use them with more intelligence. We, the GSA command of the sector 'Eastern Europe', demand results.'

'I will do my best, Mr. Chernin', promised Medschenko, gasping. He sat down again.

'It will have serious consequences for you, if you fail! A lot of us are very angry because of your policy. Think about it, and be happy that the 'Council of the Elders' has not heard about the situation in Belarus so far,' grumbled Chernin and asked for a glass of juice in the next second.

'Rely on me!' said Medschenko quietly.

*You know, we have a lot to do in Russia and the other regions of the sector. Your little Belarus or even the tiny Baltic countries are not very interesting for our leaders in Moscow. Put down this bunch of rebels and finally ensure, that larger sums of money can be extracted from this country in the future,' ordered the GSA man with a smug undertone.

'I will give my best!' promised Medschenko again.

'Do this, if you want to remain governor. My goodness, this ridiculous street preacher Tschistokjow and his rebel friends can't be stopped by you? I can only laugh about that, Mr. Medschenko,' said Chernin and went to the door.

He nodded theatrically, then he perked his eyebrows up and left the room without saying goodbye to the governor. The portly politician was left alone in his office, and was staring into space. Shortly afterwards, he grabbed a phone and dialed a number, but he let only ring it once. In a flash he ended the call and put the phone back on the table. Medschenko stood up, leaned against his desk and drummed with his fingers on the wood.

In the following months, Belarus and the Baltic countries were shaken by a wave of political agitation, while Medschenko and his apparatus of power had more and more problems to impede the Rus.

Especially in the rural regions of Belarus the Rus attacked the state authority by all available means. Dozens of representatives of Medschenko's regime were killed during a campaign Tschistokjow called 'counterterror'.

Local administrators and officials, journalists, attorneys, judges, a few unteachable policemen, notorious members of secret societies and some more fell victim to this bloody operation.

All had been organized by Peter Ulljweski and a special unit of troopers. The message behind all this was clear: The Rus were the new power in these regions and everyone, who was still standing in their way, would be destroyed.

Frank and the others were constantly on the road until the end of August. Tired and exhausted, they finally allowed themselves a short vacation. Frank had found only a bit free time in the last months; time to think about his life outside the political struggle.

Today was such a day, and he thought that he was meanwhile feeling much better. Days like this were days of musing and often ended in depression.

He cracked his brain about this and that, and came to the solution that he was only successful in one thing - fighting. Everything else was still unknown territory for him.

Frank once more listened to the village boss in Wilden's study. The former businessman was talking about new plans for another publicity campaign in the autumn and winter months. By now, Wilden was more than ever some kind of 'PR manager' for the movement, and his family only noticed him as an always babbling shadow in the background.

'Goodbye, Thorsten! Until tomorrow!' said Frank quietly and closed the door of the study.

He slowly walked down the steps to the lower floor. Before he left the house, he went into the kitchen where Agatha Wilden and Julia were sitting. Frank muttered a silent bye and wanted to leave again, he turned around.

'Wait!' he suddenly heard from behind.

Julia followed him and entered the hallway. 'How are you? Are you all right?'

'Yes, thanks for asking.'

'What's wrong with you in the last time, Frank? Why do you treat me like that?'

'Treat you like what?'

'You know what I mean.'

'No!'

'Yes, you look right through me most of the time. Are you still angry?'

Frank frowned. 'No, should I?'

'You are angry because of Viktor, aren't you?' said Julia, beholding him sadly.

'I give a shit on that guy!' growled Kohlhaas.

'Me too. You should know that I am no longer his girlfriend,' she answered.

'That's your thing. Currently, I have more important things on my mind than your love affairs,' he replied gruffly.

'Thus, I just wanted you to know.'

'I knew it anyway.'

Julia stroke through her blonde hair and was embarrassed.

'It was a mistake. Viktor has behaved like an asshole.'

Frank paused briefly and smiled. 'That's no new information for me. He is an asshole. I knew it from the first moment I saw him.'

'Do you want to go with me to Steffen's cafe tomorrow? Just to chat a bit...,' asked Julia.

'Tomorrow? That's difficult. Probably Artur will come to Ivas and we have to talk with HOK about some political things.' Frank cleared his throat.

'Well, I would be happy,' said the daughter of the village boss and returned to the kitchen with a sad face.

Frank looked after her and stood around for a moment. Then he shouted, 'If Artur doesn't come, then we could go to Steffen's cafe.'

'All right!,' it resounded out of the next room.

Frank smiled to himself and his inner self rejoiced mightily. Of course, he would never ignore this offer of the blonde beauty.

'Women are manipulative creatures from hell,' he thought with a broad smile. Finally, he walked home, still chuckling to himself.

The leader of the Rus did not come to Ivas the next day. He was somewhere in Belarus and had also never said that he wanted visit them today. Frank had gotten up early and was standing in front of the mirror in the bathroom, washing, combing, perfuming - since over one hour. Outside he heard Alf ranting.

'You're pretty enough! Now let me in, I've got to go to the loo!'

Bäumer finally stormed the bath, pushed his friend to the side and occupied the room, while Frank left him rolling his eyes.

'I go now!' he shouted from the hallway and disappeared.

Frank walked down the street and enjoyed the warm sun rays which were gently caressing his face. For some minutes he sank deeply into his thoughts, musing about what he would say to Julia today. He went into a side street and saw the yellow and red flowers in front of the house of the Wildens. Julia's mother opened the door and greeted him warmly.

'Do you want to visit Thorsten?' she asked.

'He is away with John Thorphy and will come back tomorrow.'

Frank shook his head. 'No, I want to visit Julia.'

The pretty blonde appeared in the hallway and smiled at him. 'We go to the village, mom!'

Shortly afterwards, they left. Mrs. Wilden threw a pensive look after them.

'I'm glad that you have come,' said Julia, walking beside her shy companion.

'Thus, Artur has suddenly canceled his visit,' he muttered quietly.

'I understand! What a coincidence,' returned Julia with a grin.

They were silent for a while and finally came to the village square. Some children were playing here and tried to climb up the memorial stone, which was overgrown with scrub.

'Let's go to Steffen,' suggested Julia.

'Okay!' was Frank's short answer. He was still searching for a topic to talk about.

Julia was a true feast for the eye, he thought. She wore her hair open and it was falling down her shoulders. Frank looked fascinated at Julia's red lips, while she was slowly walking in front of him.

'What are you waiting for? Come on!' she said and Frank followed her.

'She is like Lorelei - luring the poor Frank to the rocks...,' he muttered under his breath.

They crossed the square and went to the small patio outside the cafe of their Belgian friend. Frank sat down on a plastic chair and was silent.

'Ah, rare guests!' exclaimed Steffen de Vries and came towards them. 'What can I do for you?'

Julia smiled. 'I would like to have a milkshake.'

'For me too,' said Frank.

The Fleming nodded and walked off. Kohlhaas looked thoughtfully at the old church that the villagers had converted into a meeting house. He still did not have a topic to talk about with Julia.

'What's about your political struggle?' she asked then.

'Well, anything runs smoothly at the moment,' answered Frank.

'My father speaks of nothing else anymore. Revolution, revolution, revolution - here and there,' she remarked annoyed.

'Has it ever been different?'

'No, to be honest.'

'And what's about Viktor?'

She hesitated and stroke through her hair. "I don't know. I haven't heard anything from him since weeks.'

'Is it really over?'

'It is. He didn't mean it seriously.'

'I've always hated that guy!'

Julia opened her eyes. 'I've already noticed that.'

Steffen de Vries came back with two milk shakes. Frank emptied his glass with a single sip and said nothing for several minutes.

'I thought that you would go to Grodno one day, and I would never see you again,' said Frank after a pause.

'You don't have to worry about such things anymore,' replied Julia with a smile.

'Worry? I just wanted to say...,' whispered Kohlhaas meekly.

'I understand, what you mean.'

'What did he do?' asked Frank.

'He's an asshole! Not very honest,' said Julia.

'Did he cheat on you?'

'I think so. He just wasn't the right one.'

'Anyway! That is not my affair.'

'No problem!' said Julia, smiling again.

'Well, but it's nice that you're back in town.'

'I would never have left Ivas. I like our village far too much.'

Frank examined the church again, then he looked at the bottom of his glass which was covered with frothy milk. He chatted with Julia about some superficial things. After an hour, the two left the cafe and wandered around aimlessly.

'See you later! It was really nice. We should meet more often. What do you think?' she said and gave Frank a wink. Then she walked down the street.

'Yes, sure!' answered Frank and went back home too.

Soon after he had reached his house, he opened the door and disappeared inside. Frank went into his bedroom to muse about his life.

A few days later, Frank drove to Belarus and stayed there for several weeks. He tried to forget Julia and all the other private things, and distributed newspapers and leaflets, together with the other young men from Ivas. At the end of the month, the Rus demonstrated in Bresk in the south of the country. Tschistokjow had mobilized about 15000 people. Before the rally, violent clashes between Belarusians and immigrants from Asia Minor had shaken the city for days. Two men had died and several dozens had been wounded. However, the demonstration itself ended without violence. The local police did not disturb the Rus and GCF soldiers did not appear on this day.

Obviously, Medschenko and his advisers had meanwhile realized that pressure and terror were not the right methods against Tschistokjow and his followers.

In October, the Belarusian government finally announced the increase of the prices for oil and gas. A wave of anger swept across the country and the 'Freedom Movement of the Rus' reached an unknown degree of popularity.

Moreover, there were spontaneously organized strikes of steel workers in Minsk and Nowopolozk, and Medschenko had to make concessions for the first time. He finally accepted higher wages for steel workers.

'Wait until it is really cold. Then the boiler will explode!' predicted Artur in these days again and again.

And Frank and the others waited. Meanwhile, Kohlhaas also believed that they could really win.

Abnormal End

At the end of October, the 'Freedom Movement of the Rus' made its first major rally in Lithuania. Artur had chosen Vilnius, the political center of the country. At the same time, there were also smaller demonstrations in five other Lithuanian cities.

About 10000 men and women marched through the streets of Vilnius where they encountered a much more aggressive police than in Belarus. After just half an hour it ended in bloody riots and firefights.

The roughly 500 armed troopers, who were led by Frank and Peter Ulljewski, had a short shootout with the Lithuanian security forces and thirty guardsmen and several officers were killed.

Artur eventually stopped the rally before his followers had reached the inner city, and Frank and his friends from Ivas fled to Vitebsk. This time, the media of the administration sector 'Eastern Europe' reported about the failed demonstration of the Rus with their usual scorn. The newscasters spoke of 'criminals', 'terrorists' and 'rioters'.

Nevertheless, Artur and his followers were not discouraged. After all, the smaller rallies in the other Lithuanian cities had ended peacefully.

After the rally in Vilnius, also Igor, the leader of the Lithuanian section, was arrested by the police and a little later executed because of 'breach of the peace'. The media extensively reported about it again.

'That was big shit!' hissed Frank, picking in the mashed potatoes on his plate which Alf had cooked.

His friend nodded and replied, 'I won't join another demonstration in Lithuania, this is too dangerous for us. We will only attract the attention of the authorities to our village.'

'It has been Wilden's brilliant idea - once more,' grumbled Frank.

'If we would really take over the power in Belarus one day, we can also liberate Lithuania,' returned Bäumer and brought the next pot of mashed potatoes.

'How old are they anyway?' asked Frank, pointing at the steaming metal pot.

'What?'

'The potatoes! How old?'

Alfred scratched his head. 'They are from our stock in the cellar.'

Frank made a disgusted face. 'They even taste like this.'

His roommate waved his hand and left the kitchen. 'You find luxury elsewhere!'

'Will you come with me to Linda?' asked him Frank.

'Another rally?'

'No, we want to distribute newspapers.'

'Yeah, sure,' replied Alf and came back into the room.

'Anyhow, I play a bit 'Doom 8',' said Frank, putting the half-empty plate aside. Then he went into his room and booted the computer.

Wilden was again in Belarus and discussed with the inner circle of the freedom movement his plans and ideas. Guardsmen units should occupy important strategic goals in a nationwide operation when the day of revolution had come. These goals were police stations, town halls, television stations, radio stations and press houses. Furthermore, several factories and supply centers for food, water and electricity. Artur himself propagated the march on Minsk, and planned to lead his armed troopers and tens of thousands of people to the presidential palace in the inner city in order to force Medschenko to abdicate.

In the meantime, Frank, Alf, Sven and thousands of other Rus spreaded Tschistokjow's propaganda in all parts of the country.

So Frank had no more time to meet Julia in these days. Some of Artur's men were also preparing a general strike of the Belarusian workers and infiltrated numerous production complexes and factories.

At the beginning of November, there were further demonstrations in all parts of the country which were organized by the local group leaders.

Meanwhile, the police mostly avoided confrontations with the Rus. Tschistokjow himself had also ordered his followers to use violence only in emergency situations.

This brought the Rus a lot of sympathies among the frustrated policemen and the local administrators, who slowly realized, that something had to change.

Finally, the winter of 2035 came over Belarus, Lithuania and the surrounding countries like an angry nemesis. Already in December, the land was assaulted by a harsh wave of ice and snow which was tormenting millions of people. The fact that the electricity grid of the country was completely decayed, made everything even more dramatic. Thousands of homeless and poor people froze to death within a few days in the cities and villages in the Baltic countries and in Belarus. Right now, in the days of massive price increases for oil and gas, the people were haunted by cruel, freezing temperatures what caused a state of wrath and despair in millions of households.

Many Belarusians feared not to survive the cold period. In addition, the rest of the so far intact domestic economy collapsed and also the transport system broke down, as a result of the massive snowfalls.

It was the state of hopelessness and despair which Artur and his followers had always hoped for. The rebel leader called the upcoming cold snap, with a certain cynicism, a 'gift of God'.

Hundreds of thousands of people, who had so far remained quiet and had not openly shown their discontent, were now driven into the arms of the Rus by freezing temperatures and social hardship. The winter whipped them out of their lethargy and literally forced them to show their colors.

At first, Artur went to Moghilev where he held a demonstration with more than 50000 people, who had mostly come from the city and the surrounding villages and small towns. The freezing and starving crowd besieged the city hall and attacked the police. This time, the armed guardsmen had a lot of problems to maintain peace, but finally prevented another street fight.

Some Belarusian policemen even joined the march at the end because they suffered more and more under the lack of salary payments and the rising prices for food, oil and gas. In the middle of December, the situation became still worse. The onset of winter was so extreme that the food supply collapsed in some parts of Belarus. Frank, Alfred and their comrades took the opportunity to spread the propaganda of their political leader even more vigorously, hammering the slogans of the revolution into the heads of the despaired. Finally, armed units of the Rus took over the power in many villages and smaller towns in the north of the country - with the connivance of the local police and the authorities that partly joined the rebellion.

The mayor of Vitebsk was lynched by an angry mob in front of his house, a few days before Christmas. One week later, Tschistokjow came to the city and spoke in front of almost 30000 people. The local police accepted his march through the streets and avoided any conflicts.

Meanwhile, Medschenko had already lost control over the situation. In Moscow, St. Petersburg, Kiev and other cities in Russia and the Ukraine it also came to riots and hunger revolts which could be quelled by the security forces after a few days.

Any Christmas parties and the New Year's festival were canceled in Ivas this time, because most inhabitants of the village were helping the Rus and supported their nationwide propaganda campaign.

Now, the Belarusian capital had to be taken. The time seemed to be ripe for the march on Minsk, Artur was dreaming about since years.

'The new year must end with the victory of the revolution!' repeated the rebel leader incessantly.

So they took up all their energy, their hatered and their hope to begin the all-important, large-scale attack on the wavering regime in January 2036.

Frank yawned and crawled out of his bed. Since two days he was back in Ivas and tried to enjoy some free days. Last night the snow had covered the village with a giant white sheet. They were completely snowed in.

'Damn!' whispered Frank and looked out the window.

Ice flowers covered the glass and blocked the view at the small garden behind the house which had been smothered under a thick blanket of snow.

'Now we are trapped in this dump,' he heard a voice behind him.

It was Alf. Bäumer was shivering from cold and trudged to the old wood fired oven in the living room.

'What a mess! I've never seen so much snow in my whole life. I hope our roof won't crush down sometime,' muttered Frank, entering the kitchen.

The two men drank a coffee and looked at each other in silence. After a while they felt the upcoming heat, which was crawling out of the living room to the still cold kitchen, giving the room a tolerable temperature.

'The revolution must start without us!' joked Frank and looked for something to eat.

Suddenly he startled up. Someone was knocking at the door.

'Yes, we are already here. Take it easy!' roared Bäumer annoyed and hurried down the hallway.

'Alf, thank God, you are at home! Let me in!' Frank heard a familiar voice behind the front door.

It was Wilden. The village boss was exhausted and confused, his clothes were wet and he was staring into space while Frank came nearer.

'They got Julia!' he said and ran into the kitchen. 'Do you understand? They know everything!'

201

Frank and Alf looked at each other, not knowing what to say. 'Thorsten? Are you okay?'

'They have my little angel, the GSA!' stammered the gray-haired man, gasping for breath.

'What are you talking about, Thorsten?'

'Julia has driven to Grodno - three days ago. She wanted to meet Viktor, I don't know any details. This morning, a call, the GSA! They got my Julia!' lamented Wilden. Frank spat a big splash of coffee on the table and almost fell out of his chair.

'What? Are you kidding...?'

'The GSA has called me this morning, telling me that they have kidnapped Julia. They know about me and my influence on Artur Tschistokjow. They know everything about us - and Ivas! Damn!'

Alf eyes almost fell out of his skull, Frank was chalky white and puffed quietly.

'I hope you are kidding, Thorsten! This can't be true!'

'No! This is not a stupid joke! It's the truth! I swear it!' cried Wilden.

His facial expression did not look as if he was joking. Wilden's eyes stared around in sheer horror, then he began to wail. Frank and Alf offered him a chair and he sank down, totally exhausted. Finally, Wilden started to cry and incoherently stammered something. Frank had never seen him in a condition like this before.

'This is a fucking nightmare! God!' muttered Alf, holding his head.

After a while, Wilden was able to describe the situation, more or less understandable. Apparently, Julia had driven to Grodno after Viktor had asked her to forgive him and had invited her to some kind of 'peace talk'.

In spite of the dangerous weather she had accepted Viktor's offer and had immediately driven off. Since then, Mr. and Mrs. Wilden had not heard anything from her. Until this morning, when Wilden had taken a disturbing phone call.

Someone, who had introduced himself as a GSA agent, had told Wilden that they had kidnapped his daughter. He had described her appearance in detail and a few minutes later Julia had been allowed to talk to her father.

'That's the truth!' wailed Wilden and tore his hair. 'I haven't forbidden her to drive to Grodno. God, I'm such an idiot! This weather is dangerous enough! God!'

'Why Julia?' asked Alf with confusion.

'These swines know about me! They observe us since some months, and they seem to know everything about Ivas. Above all, about me. That guy from the GSA has told me that they know about my big influence on Tschistokjow. Furthermore, they are informed that Artur is planning a march on Minsk.'

'And what shall you do for them now?' asked Frank.

'I shall dissuade Artur from the march on Minsk!' cried Wilden, banging on the table.

'Dissuade?'

'Artur mostly heeds my strategic advice, you know that. I shall confuse him, make him indecisive and tell him that the attempt to conquer Minsk is madness. Moreover, I shall stop the financing of the freedom movement immediately. I have managed it with a lot of secret accounts yet.'

'I can't believe it,' stammered Frank, holding his head totally overwhelmed.

'If I don't cooperate, they will kill Julia!' said Wilden.

'Those bastards!' growled Alf and smashed his cup against the wall.

Frank tried to think clearly and nervously scratched the back of his head. 'How do they know all this?'

'To hell! I can't say!' lamented the village boss.

'She wanted to visit Viktor?' muttered Frank, while his face contorted itself in rage.

'Yes, Viktor, yes,' sobbed Wilden.

Then Frank hissed, 'More exactly please, Thorsten!'

'How many times has Viktor actually been in Ivas?' inquired Alfred.

'Several times! He often stayed with us. He wasn't very interested in politics, this was my impression. Anyway, we didn't talk very much,' answered Wilden.

'But he still leads the group in Grodno, right?' said Kohlhaas in wonder.

'More or less, he has meanwhile given the leadership to another man and wanted to retire into private life. I just don't know more details. Shit!'

'I thought that Julia and Viktor had agreed to part ways?' grumbled Frank and was fuming with rage inside.

'Yes, I thought so too. I have no idea what is going on in Julia's head. These GSA men must have observed her for a while...,' replied Wilden and continued wailing.

Alf angrily looked at Frank. 'Do you suspect Viktor? This is nonsense! He isn't responsible for all this!'

'I haven't said that!' said Frank and turned around.

'What shall I do now?' Wilden broke out into tears again.

'Where does Viktor live? Do you have an address?'

'Oh, Frank! Yes, somewhere at home. I think, Agatha has his address. After all, he has visited us several times. Yes, we must find...'

Frank put on a coat and dragged the whining Wilden out of the house on the street, Alf followed him.

'Come on! We will need you!'

Bäumer wondered and did not really know what to do now, while Frank and the village boss walked through the high snow towards Wilden's house. It took over an hour until Agatha Wilden had calmed down a bit; again and again she was sobbing and whimpering silently. Fortunately, however, she had kept the address of Viktor.

'I need to go to Grodno!' shouted Frank while Wilden was whining quietly.

'To Grodno? How do you want to do that? There is a whole meter of snow on the roads which lead out of Ivas. Since last night, nobody can leave this village anymore,' sniveled Agatha.

'Maybe by plane!' answered Kohlhaas and waved Wilden and his wife nearer.

'Maybe...,' muttered the village boss desperately.

'Follow me!' said Frank and opened the front door.

Then he walked down the snow-covered street. Wilden was trudging after him.

Steffen de Vries, the Fleming with the reddish beard, looked a little baffled when he had to leave the breakfast table, because Frank and Wilden had yelled something in front of his house. He opened the door. Kohlhaas explained the situation with all necessary urgency and the horrified Belgian followed his orders. Wilden was silent and just whimpered quietly.

'Flying? In this weather? This is more than dangerous, Frank,' remarked Steffen.

'I know, but it doesn't snow right now, this might be a chance to get out here. You just have to bring me out of the village, then I will get to Grodno on my own,' said Frank, and also tried to reassure Steffen de Vries.

'This is risky!' muttered the Fleming.

'You will do it!' shouted Wilden and the thick Belgian cringed.

'I will call Alf and get my gun and my cell phone. See you soon!'

Frank raced through the snow as fast as he could and finally came back with Bäumer, who was still overwhelmed with the situation.

Shortly afterwards, Steffen de Vries brought the two men to Varena. When Alf told him that the village community was no secret anymore the Flemish family father was horror-struck and remained silent for the rest of the flight.

From Varena Frank and Alf finally continued their trip to Grodno by train. They arrived at the city in the early evening and found a place to sleep in a small guesthouse.

'Basically, the stupid cow hasn't deserved anything else,' growled Alf and went to bed.

'I'm do this mainly for Thorsten and the revolution,' answered Frank and yawned.

'A likely story, Kohlhaas!'

'Do you want to start an argument with me before we go to sleep?' grumbled Frank angrily.

'Thus, I'm doing it only for the revolution and not for that stupid bimbo!' scolded Alf.

'She is no bimbo!'

Alf grinned cynically. 'Nevertheless, your beloved Valkyrie has behaved like one.'

'Anyhow, the revolution must come now, otherwise we are all fucked up,' said Frank with concern.

'I know. This is nothing but a nightmare.'

They talked for another hour and had to force themselves to sleep. The fears and sorrows were sticking much too deep in their minds. Today, they had learned that their warm and safe nest, the little village of Ivas, was no longer a secret. And troubles with the GSA were no fun at all. It was a disaster.

'This is the Staraya Ulitsa!' said Frank, pointing at a rusty street sign.

'Viktor lives in number 117. Finally, Grodno is pretty big - and really ugly,' answered Alf and fetched his DC-stick.

Some minutes later, they reached a gray apartment block. A huge pile of snow was on the edge of the sidewalk and a lot of blue garbage bags were standing in front of the exterior wall.

Frank pressed a bell button and waited for a short moment, then the entrance door opened with a hum. They went up the stairs to the fourth floor. Someone was yelling in Russian on the hallway. It was Viktor. Frank ran towards him. The athletic man looked a bit puzzled at first, but then he put on a smile.

'Hey, Viktor! I'm Frank. Can you remember me?'

Alf came from behind and welcomed the young man too.

'Yes, hello Frank! And hello Alf! What are you doing here in Grondo?'

'We have to ask you a few things. Can we come in?' said Frank. Viktor stared suspiciously at him.

He hesitated for some seconds and looked around. Finally he nodded. 'Yes! Sure! Come in, my friends!'

They followed him and sat down in a beautiful furnished living room. Viktor disappeared in a side room.

'Do you want to drink something?' they heard.

'No, thanks!' answered Frank and Alf in unison.

The Belarusian came back, sat down in a chair and lit a cigarette. 'What can I do for you?'

'We are looking for Julia! Her father, Thorsten Wilden, has told us that she has gone to Grodno - to visit you,' said Frank.

Viktor looked at him thoughtfully and scraped with his fingers over the leather of the armchair. Then he answered sadly, 'Yes, Julia wanted to visit me, but she never came. Where is she?'

'She did not come to you, Viktor?' asked Alf.

'No! I'm still waiting for her, my friends. I wanted to talk to her. We are no couple anymore, just good friends...'

'Just good friends!' muttered Frank and nodded, staring at the ceiling.

'I'm full of sorrow now! Damn!' remarked Viktor.

'Same here!' said Frank.

The handsome young man waved his hand and made a sad impression.

'I can not help you, my friends. Sorry!'

Frank and Alfred looked at each other and did not answer him.

'Shit!' hissed Kohlhaas.

Then Viktor talked with them about all kinds of unimportant things and asked them to tell Julia that she should immediately give him a sign when she reappeared. Suddenly, the Belarusian stood up and went to the toilet.

His two guests remained on the sofa, totally frustrated. Frank scratched his chin.

'Do you think that he is telling the truth?' he asked his friend.

'Why should he tell us crap?'

'I don't trust him.'

'You hate him because Julia still seems to like him.'

'Well, maybe you're right. Anyway, he can't help us. We should go.'

Meanwhile, Alf had put is forefinger in a narrow gap between the seat cushions of the sofa, moving it back and forth absentmindedly. After a while, he sensed a tiny piece of paper and pulled it out. Frank had closed his eyes and looked tired.

'The disaster takes its course. It was all in vain,' he thought and let out a sigh.

In the meantime, Alf tried to decipher the Cyrillic text on the piece of paper which he had pulled out of the gap between the seat cushions. It was a receipt of a gas station, from 06.01.2036.

'Vladimir Zolinski, gas station, Prienai,' he read out quietly.

Alf crumpled up the little piece of paper, without thinking.

A toilet flushing resounded, while Bäumer put the receipt into his coat pocket. Viktor came back into the living room.

'Thanks! We have to go now!' explained Frank and they went to the door.

'Okay! I hope Julia is all right,' returned Viktor. He shook their hands.

After a few minutes, they had almost reached the entrance door of the apartment block. Frank kicked angrily against the banister and Alf was musing.

'What a mess! We'll never find her!' muttered Kohlhaas and looked at his friend.

A heartbeat later Bäumer stopped, he took a deep breath and hastily scrabbled in the pocket of his coat.

'What are you doing?' asked Frank.

'Wait!'

Alf finally pulled out the crumpled-up piece of paper and stared at it. He was heavily breathing.

'Today is the 10th of January, right?'

'Yes! Why?' returned Frank. 'What's up?'

'This is a receipt of a gas station. It is dated on 06.01.2036 - three days ago. I have found it between the cushions of Viktor's sofa.'

'So fucking what? Don't waste my time with this!'

'Somebody has tanked up his car at the gas station in Prienai. This is the first gas station you reach, if you come from Ivas and drive further towards the highway.'

'Yes, I know that gas station, but...?' replied Kohlhaas casually.

'But why was this receipt between the cushions of Viktor's sofa?'

Frank winced and stumbled against the banister. He looked at Alf with mouth agape and was dumbfounded.

March on Minsk

Frank and Alf had gone back to their motel room. Bäumer was trying to calm Frank who was raging like a mad bull.

'I'm going to beat the shit out of this guy!' he ranted.

'Start thinking, Frank! We need another strategy!' said Alf.

'That bastard is a traitor! He is working for the GSA! I gonna kill him!'

'Now stop this shit! Get a grip! We must keep cool!' answered Alf, touching Frank's shoulder.

Kohlhaas growled quietly and muttered some curses. Alf suddenly came to him and said, 'We lie in wait and shadow Viktor. Perhaps we will find out something.'

'Shadow him? I will cut his treacherous throat!' hissed Frank.

'Yes, run around, scream and shoot - idiot!' replied Alf.

They finally left the motel and positioned themselves in a doorway near Viktor's apartment block. Several times, Bäumer had to stop his hot-blooded friend who wanted to kick in the entrance door and attack the Belarusian. Both men waited until the evening and were freezing. But Viktor did not show up.

On the next day they had more luck. The Belarusian came out of his house around noon, and Frank and Alf followed him quietly through some streets.

Eventually, Viktor stopped and went into another apartment block. Frank and Alfred sneaked after him and tried to keep him in sight. An elderly woman, walking on crutches, let him in. Viktor welcomed her warmly and finally went inside. Frank and Alf stalked after him and listened at the door.

'It's his mother. He has used the word 'Matj', hasn't he?' whispered Kohlhaas.

They hid in a dark corner near the door. After about an hour, Viktor left the apartment again. The old woman hobbled after him, still chatting loudly in Russian. Then Viktor walked down to the entrance of the house. Alf had to retain Frank once more.

When they were back in the motel, Frank walked nervously through the room and Alf looked at him, shaking his head.

'And now?'

'Great! Now we know where Viktor's mother lives,' growled Kohlhaas. 'We should grab that guy and have another small talk. I swear, I will make him talk!'

'Use your brain, Frank!' moaned Bäumer and sat down on his bed.

'What's next?' grumbled Frank.

'I have a better idea. Mrs. Wilden has given you Viktor's phone number, right?'

'Yes, she has! So what?'

'We'll do another thing! It is mean, but we are dealing here with the GSA and therefore we have also to be nasty.'

Frank frowned. 'What do you mean?'

'I'll explain it to you...,' said Alf.

Meanwhile, they were already sitting and waiting in the basement of the apartment building since hours. It was getting dark outside.

'What time is it?' whispered Frank.

'It's 21:34 pm...,' answered Bäumer.

'Okay, let's go!'

They hurried upstairs and looked around nervously, then they sneaked down the hallway of the third floor. Frank listened at the door of the apartment. Inside, they heard the noise of a TV. Kohlhaas knocked on the door and looked at Alf while a quiet rumbling came out of the apartment.

'Kto sdjes?' asked Viktor's mother.

Frank cleared his throat and tried to sound friendly. He explained in a few words that he was a friend of Viktor and was searching for him. For half a minute, the two men heard no sound, then the door was opened and a kind, old lady looked out.

'Viktor nje doma.'

She was interrupted in the next second. Alf came from the side, pushed her back into the apartment and pressed his hand on her mouth. Frank closed the door and held his gun under the nose of the terrified woman. She started to moan anxiously while Alf dragged her into the living room and told her to be quiet. Shortly afterwards, Frank dialed Viktor's phone number and waited.

'Da! Sdjes Viktor!'

'Hello! It's me! Frank Kohlhaas from Ivas!'

'Hey, Frank! What's up?'

'Tell me where Julia is, Viktor! Where did the GSA men bring her?' growled Frank into the phone.

'What GSA men?' asked Viktor with surprise.

'Don't tell me shit, Viktor! I know that Julia has visited you!'

'What? She has never been here!' answered the young man at the other end of the line.

'Viktor, we know that she has visited you. Now tell me where she is!' barked Frank into the receiver.

'I don't know what you want, idiot! Fuck you!' nagged Viktor and replaced.

Frank called him again and this time the Belarusian was really angry.

'What the fuck do you want from me, Frank?'

Kohlhaas was fuming with rage. 'Do you hear that?'

'Pomogai mne, Viktor! Pashalusta!' wailed the old woman when Alf held the phone in front of her mouth.

'What the hell...?' stammered Viktor.

'We got your mother! Tell me where Julia is or we will kill her! This is no joke!' threatened Frank.

Viktor seemed to be shocked and whispered something in Russian. Then he was silent.

'If you hurt her, I will kill you, Frank!' he yelled then.

Frank stayed calm and answered, 'Okay, we make a deal. We know that you are a traitor. But I give a shit on that. Just tell me where the GSA has brought Julia. Then we let your mother go.'

Alf finally took the phone and gave it to the old woman, who was begging her son for help, crying all the time.

Then Frank continued to talk with Viktor again and stressed that he and Alf would immediately kill his mother, if he did not cooperate.

Suddenly, Viktor started to wail too, and told him that the GSA had forced him to become an informer.

'They have forced you to do it?' said Frank. 'I don't believe a single word. But I don't care about that. You must live with it, not me. Now tell me where Julia is!'

Viktor explained him that the GSA men had brought her to a hotel in the south of the city. A few minutes later, Frank had all the necessary information.

'If you lie to me, call the police or tell someone anything, Alf will kill your mother!' hissed Frank into the receiver, put back and left the apartment.

While Alfred was taking care of Viktor's mother and tried to calm the crying woman somehow, Frank was already on his way to the southern part of Grodno. A taxi brought him to the hotel and he got out of the car in a side street. Soon after Frank had reached a big, dark building.

'Room 32, Floor 5...,' he whispered under his breath and reached for the weapon under his jacket.

Frank put on a black baseball cap, trying to hide his face as best as he could, and went inside.

A young woman at the reception briefly smiled at him and asked something in Russian, but Kohlhaas just nodded and tried to smile too. Finally, he ran up the staircase.

Meanwhile, it was 23:15 pm. An old man met him on the stairs. Frank murmured a greeting and peered down the dimly lit corridor of the 5th floor.

Nobody seemed to be here. Somewhere behind the door next to him he heard a television. Frank remained pensive for a few minutes and waited in a dark corner.

'It must go quickly now!' he said to himself and screwed a silencer on his gun.

A minute later, he sneaked to the door of room 32 and took a deep breath. The adrenaline was burning in his veins and his heart started to pound wildly. Frank closed his eyes, looked around for a last time and took aim at the door lock.

'Pffft! Pffft!'

Little splinters of wood flew around and he gained access to the dark room with a powerful kick.

'Kto sdjes?' he heard out of a corner and a man in a brown leather jacket came out of the darkness.

Frank shot him directly in the head and jumped forward. In the corner of his eye he could see Julia who had been bound to a chair. She was staring at him with wide eyes.

'Frank!' she yelled.

'Wait!'

'Frank! Behind you!'

Kohlhaas turned around in a flash and recognized another man, who was coming out of the shower room next to him. The GSA agent pulled a gun and tried to take aim at him with a terrified look. Frank stepped to the side and fired wildly around. A bullet hit his opponent in the shoulder and the man staggered backwards, screaming in pain. Frank continued to shoot at him until the GSA man slid down the bloodstained wall.

'There's another one! He is out to fetch cigarettes and will come back in the next minutes. I can't believe that you...,' stammered Julia excitedly.

'We must take to our heels!' gasped Frank, cutting the fetters with his knife and leading Julia out of the hotel room. They ran down the stairs and passed a group of surprised looking hotel guests. Then they disappeared in the dark streets of Grodno. Frank called Alf immediately.

Bäumer apologized to Viktor's mother for the inconveniences and finally left her alone. During the night, Frank and Julia hid in a vacant building and met him in the early morning hours. They stole a car and drove back to Kaunas in Lithuania.

Steffen de Vries picked them up with his plane and brought them back to their snowbound home village. Thorsten Wilden and his wife could not believe it. They were besides themselves with joy when they held their only child in their arms again. Frank had never seen Wilden so happy before. He was crying like a child and could hardly put his gratitude into words.

Frank was once again the hero for all, and the whole village paid homage to him - so much that Frank was almost swamped with it. Julia seemed to idolize him now and he could rightly claim that he had finally won her heart with this rescue mission.

Now, Frank had conquered the pretty woman, but he still remained restrained and uncertain. The praise, coming from all sides, and Julia's adoring glances made him feel more confused than inspired. So he avoided to meet her in the following days, and did not really know why.

'Maybe I'm only suitable for combat. Peace and love are still foreign to me,' he said to himself.

The month had come to an end. Cold and hunger were tormenting the people of Belarus like never before as chaos and anarchy were spreading at breakneck speed in the big cities. Food stores were stormed by hungry crowds and sometimes the looters slayed each other for the last piece of bread. Artur finally decided that the time was ripe to risk everything.

On 01.02.2036, he gave his followers the order to attack the government of the sub-sector 'Belarus-Baltic' by all means. On the following morning, his armed units began to form combat groups and officially took over the most small towns of the country.

The majority of police stations was occupied without bloodshed and the officers were disarmed. Often the Belarusian policemen even went over to the Rus. Meanwhile, the leaders of the freedom movement mustered their supporters and organized protest marches and rallies, which propagated Artur Tschistokjow's takeover.

Administration buildings, press agencies, radio and broadcasting stations were captured at first in the smaller towns and cities. Where the servants of the World Government tried to oppose, the rebels put them down with brutal resoluteness, showing them that they were ready for anything. In some small towns, even the local police helped the Rus to oust the political opponents. At the same time, the big cities of Belarus were shaken by riots and strikes. Moreover, hundreds of thousands of workers had laid down their work and had banded together, either spontaneously or under the direct guidance of members of the freedom movement.

However, Artur put his focus on Minsk. If he would fail to conquer the capital and to force Medschenko to resign, then the successes in the smaller cities would be meaningless in the long term.

So Artur finally sent his trooper units to Minsk and his men gathered in the vicinity of the capital. Countless Belarusians joined the great march, in spite of the freezing cold, and were now waiting for the signal to advance. Frank commanded a trooper unit of over 3000 men who had gathered in Zdanovicy. Alf steadfastly remained at his side - as always.

After an uncomfortable night of hungering and freezing, the guardsmen units started to move towards Minsk, in the gray of dawn of 04.02.2036.

Meanwhile, Medschenko's last loyal helpers, the GCF occupation troops and some police squads, had sealed off the capital and especially the government district. All in all it were almost 15000 soldiers, and the policemen who had not changed sides yet.

Thousands of rebels were marching across closed highways and access roads. They came by car, by foot, with trucks or even occupied trains. Many of them were equipped with modern firearms, others had just axes, iron bars or clubs. On Wilden's advice, Artur had told his men to occupy strategically important places which were responsible for the water and electricity supply of the capital. Here, it came to the first firefights of the day.

The sun was slowly rising on the horizon, but just a few rays came through the gray cloud cover. It was incredibly cold and lightly snowing. The merciless frost had tormented the men during the whole night. Most of them had not eaten something because the rations were largely depleted. But Frank ignored his growling stomach as best as he could.

The Belarusian troopers started to sing a song and some of them held dragon head flags in their frozen hands. Frank marched at the head of the column. Alf walked beside him and gave him a tired smile.

'I suggest to make the next revolution in the summer months,' he joked.

219

Frank just nodded and rolled his eyes. From afar, he could see the outlines of Minsk in the twilight of the morning. The capital was still a fair way off.

The marching column moved forward on a broad asphalt street. Several cars had been parked on the roadside and occasionally some people waved at them. Others joined the gray uniformed crowd and started to sing too. Three big trucks drove past them. It were a few dozen Rus who were cheering loudly, holding their flags out the windows. On one of the cars was a stationary machine gun and a group of freezing men had gathered around it.

After an hour, they had reached the outskirts of Minsk. It was snowing heavily now, some of the Rus started to curse. As they moved through a prefab neighborhood, hundreds of citizens joined the marching column and within a short time about 2000 people followed the guardsmen.

'If it goes belly-up today...,' worried Frank.

'We must conquer this city. There is no more turning back now,' said Alf with stoic composure.

Shortly afterwards, Frank stopped the column and called Artur. Meanwhile, more and more people were joining the crowd, they were cheering and screaming loudly.

'Where are you now?' asked Frank.

'I'm in the south of Minsk. We are still waiting for some other groups,' answered Tschistokjow.

'How many are you?'

'Maybe about 30000 people!'

'That is a lot! Sounds good!'

'It's still morning, Frank. Many thousands of people will still come. We will get much support from the people in Minsk.'

After the phone call Frank felt a bit more confident. He shouted some orders and the column continued to move forward.

'Today Tschistokjow will liberate our country!' chanted the crowd and still more people came out of their houses. 'The meeting point is in front of the security zone, near the presidential palace in the inner city. Artur says that many of our men are still on their way,' said Frank.

Some the citizens brought the rebels food. Frank ordered a short rest, then they marched on. The troopers had still some kilometers to walk and it was exhausting and arduous, apart from the growing tension that slowly took over the minds of the men.

The column marched down a long shopping street, crossed another prefab neighborhood and stopped at a large square, where it was awaited by thousands of screaming people. It took about two hours until they had finally reached the inner city.

Meanwhile, Minsk was slowly awaking. Men and women were gathering on the streets, yelling, singing - and willing to end Medschenko's reign today. When Frank and his men arrived at the presidential palace, they saw a giant crowd. Frank had never seen so many people in his whole life. It were tens of thousands.

'It's 11:00 am now. This looks encouraging!' exclaimed Frank confidently.

'Somewhere in this crowd must be Wilden and the others,' returned Alf.

'Artur has told me that the rally will start at 13:00 am. We still have two hours.'

Countless men and women were clogging the streets of the inner city to the last corner. In the meantime, the GCF soldiers had positioned themselves around the presidential palace and in some outlying districts. They were now facing not only the ordinary Belarusians, but also the renegade policemen, who had come in their uniforms to support Tschistokjow's rebellion.

When the Belarusian rebel leader finally started his speech at 13:00 am, he stood in front of more than 400000 people.

'How may he feel now?' thought Frank and held his breath.

The GCF soldiers behaved quietly so far, they tried to encircle the huge mass as good as possible. Thunderous applause and chants let the asphalt shake, countless flags were waved while Tschistokjow was staring at the giant crowd. Then it began.

'Belarusians, compatriots! Today, I have come to Minsk to dethrone the traitor Medschenko and his servants! And you will help me to end his tyranny!'

The crowd screamed and cheered. Artur went on with his ardent speech and accused the government with cutting words. He demanded that the GCF soldiers should lay down their weapons immediately to give him access to the presidential palace.

'At the end of this day our country will finally be free!' he shouted into the microphone.

The protesters screamed even louder, while more and more people came from everywhere to see Tschistokjow. Then Artur gave the sub-governor an ultimatum to resign, till 15:00 pm.

'Give me the power now, Mr. Medschenko! Otherwise, the enslaved people of Belarus will storm your residence to get their freedom! Don't challenge us anymore! Your time is over, Mr. Medschenko!' called Tschistokjow at the top of his lungs.

'Tanks!'

Alf pointed at some of the scary vehicles which were moving towards the crowd from afar.

'At 14:30 pm, our unit will attack the GCF soldiers in the restricted area at the east side of the palace,' said Frank.

Kohlhaas called the leaders of the trooper squads together. They should wait for his sign and should stay away from the crowd.

'We have some bazookas, if tanks or Skydragons appear,' he explained.

'What's about Peter Ulljewski?'

'He leads the other assault force that will attack the palace from the west. The rest comes from the front. If Medschenko doesn't give up, we will have no other choice than attacking the GCF troops.'

After Frank had said these words, he felt the anxiety growing inside him. He became aware of the fact that they had to succeed today, otherwise the revolt would fail in the long term.

'We'll crush these rats - they or us!' hissed Alf and clenched his fist.

Then he went to the troopers in order to give them further instructions. While Artur inspired the people with a revolutionary frenzy and preached about the coming age of freedom and justice, the minutes passed without mercy.

Nobody could tell anymore how many people had meanwhile gathered around the security zone. During the last hour more and more had come, and many of them had armed themselves with everything they could get. A peaceful victory seemed to become increasingly unlikely.

As the clock showed 14:30, Frank, Alfred and 3000 armed guardsmen marched in a wide arc towards the eastern area of the presidential palace.

From a distance, they could hear Artur Tschistokjow's angry voice, heating up the crowd which responded with loud cheers and screams. When Frank and his troopers moved through a side street, they came upon about 200 police officers, who raised their hands up and laid down their weapons. Frank ordered 50 of his men to guard them; the rest of the unit marched forward. A few minutes later, his watch showed him that the ultimatum had expired.

'Mr. Medschenko! We all hope that you are sensible enough to come out of the presidential palace now to give me the rule over Belarus. I'll give you another quarter of an hour. Resign - and this day will end without bloodshed. I also promise to spare you, though you do not deserve it!' shouted Tschistokjow defiantly.

But even these minutes passed without any reaction of Medschenko because the sub-governor had already escaped from Minsk two days ago, and had left it to the GCF and the police to protect the presidential palace. Meanwhile, he was in Moscow to seek asylum.

'The time is up! Now, the people of Belarus will take their freedom by force!' heard Frank the leader of the Rus call in the background.

The crowd roared and shots were fired. It became bloody. 'Follow me!' shouted Frank and waved his men nearer.

They ran forward and started to fire immediately, while the first GCF soldiers became visible behind a barricade.

The rebels attacked them with loud screams, several hand grenades detonated. Frank and Alf jumped behind a car. The numerically superior Belarusians swarmed out and attacked the GCF soldiers behind the barricades from two sides. Frank crawled to a car while he heard bullets hitting the sheet of the vehicle.

Alf hurled a hand grenade and ripped a hole into the barricade in front of him. Some GCF soldiers ran screaming out of a cloud of smoke.

With a loud war cry the troopers rushed forward, fired at their enemies and slaughtered them in a brutal shooting and stabbing. One of the rebels even had a flamethrower on his back and unleashed a fiery jet upon the soldiers behind the cover.

'They're trying to backtrack towards the palace!' shouted Frank and shot a GCF soldier in the back.

He looked around. A few dozen rebels were dead or wounded. The rest was running forward, shouting loudly. Suddenly a heavy machine gun salvo pounded through the swarm of the charging troopers.

'Damn! Four of these tanks!' shouted Alf and hit the dirt. The rolling monsters came from behind the presidential palace and shot at everyone in their way. Frank jumped like a cat behind a barricade. One of the tanks was destroyed by a bazooka, but the other vehicles unwaveringly rolled forward, mowing down a group of Rus.

'Who has anti-tank mines?' yelled Frank at some Belarusians.

A young man next to him anxiously shrugged his shoulders. Kohlhaas dragged him behind the barrier and rummaged his backpack.

'Look! This is an anti-tank mine!' he hissed and held a limpet mine under the nose of the trooper.

A second armored vehicle detonated a few meters away from him after another bazooka hit. Nevertheless, more and more troopers tried to escape from the dreaded vehicles.

Frank jumped behind one of the armored beasts and heard a machine gun salvo sweeping over his head. He fixed the mine at the rear part of the tank, which exploded shortly thereafter with a loud bang.

Then the bazookas also destroyed the last enemy vehicle. They had finally taken the eastern part of the security zone.

Shortly afterwards, the rebels occupied the barricades which the GCF soldiers had built before. Now they had even conquered several heavy machine guns. During the next hour they stopped a counterattack of the GCF and finally drove the enemy back towards the palace.

While Frank and his comrades struggled through the curtain fire of the defenders, Peter Ulljewski's men, at the opposite side, were in a bloody firefight too. In the meantime, the large crowd tried to storm the presidential palace from the front.

Tens of thousands of roaring, raging Belarusians clashed against the GCF soldiers in front the huge building, while hundreds of men and women died in a murderous hail of bullets. It was a slaughter. Within seconds, the first attackers fell down, screaming, bleeding and dying, but the onrushing crowd behind them was in such frenzy that it could not be stopped anymore.

The greatest part of the Belarusian policemen, who had followed the commands of the sub-governor so far, was seized by panic in the face of this carnage and fled or surrendered. Many of them were lynched by the furious citizens or shot down by Tschistokjow's troopers. Finally, the remaining GCF soldiers ran back into the palace or fled too.

Frank gave his men the order to get through the side entrance of the huge building and the rebels stormed forward. Some GCF soldiers fired out the windows and killed several troopers.

'Give it to me!' yelled Alf, he pulled a bazooka out of a trooper's hand and fired at one of the front windows.

A deafening bang followed and concrete parts rained down on the heads of the men. Other Rus attacked the GCF soldiers in the building with grenade launchers.

Finally, the troopers stormed the eastern part of the palace and mowed down everyone in their way with furious bursts. Frank jumped over the dead body of a comrade, who was riddled with bullets. He threw a hand grenade into a side room.

After a deafening detonation, three wounded GCF soldiers staggered out of a cloud of smoke, tumbling directly in front of the muzzle of Frank's weapon. He shot them down and looked grimly around to seek further enemies. Now he heard shots and screams, coming from the entrance of the presidential palace, while his troopers struggled through the chaos, trying to reach the next corridor.

Meanwhile, the angry crowd was pouring through the magnificent entrance hall of the building and overpowered a group of enemy soldiers. Then they smashed everything around them to pieces in their unbridled fury.

Artur stared at scenario in front of him. Dozens of dead and wounded men were lying everywhere in the hall. Suddenly, a soldier at the end of the ornate staircase, which led to the upper floor, was waving a white flag.

'Okay! We give up!' he shouted.

Some armed troopers pointed their guns at him but Artur held them back.

'Everyone of you, who stops fighting now, will not be killed!' replied Tschistokjow.

The GCF soldier and a bigger number of his comrades finally came down the stairs and took the opportunity to surrender.

Many raging citizens spat at them or tried to beat them. The troopers had a lot of problems to stop the angry crowd from lynching the hated occupiers. Frank and the survivors of his unit came into the hall and finally found Artur. The blond man smiled and embraced Frank with tears in his eyes.

'We have finally won!' he gasped wearily.

'Yes, the presidential palace is taken!' called Frank and raised his fist. The people around him cheered in a flush of victory.

Artur Tschistokjow let the surviving GCF soldiers herd together and guard by his troopers. Then he walked up the stairs and down a long corridor which was adorned with wall hangings and old paintings. Artur smiled and finally reached the office of the sub-governor.

His men followed him and started to sing the hymn of the freedom movement. Shortly thereafter, Tschistokjow took a dragon head flag from one of his guardsmen, opened the window and waved it in front of the huge screaming crowd below him. He closed his eyes. Tens of thousands of men and women were shouting his name - again and again.

Frank and Alf stood beside him and looked at the endless sea of people which was covering the whole inner city of Minsk.

Finally, Wilden, who had a laceration on his forehead, entered the room too. The gray haired village boss was weeping for joy, and for a short moment he looked like a happy, young man again.

Beacon of Hope

Artur Tschistokjow was worshiped by the people like a newly crowned king and proclaimed the re foundation of the Belarusian state. Meanwhile, his men controlled the radio and TV stations in the country and spread the message of the revolution to the last corner of Belarus.

Thorsten Wilden was the foreign minister in Tschistokjow's new cabinet. Frank was solemnly appointed as a 'General of the Army of Belarus'.

Piece by piece, the Rus took over the power in all regions of the land and after a few weeks they controlled the entire administration and the media. Furthermore, thousands of servants of the fallen regime were arrested by Tschistokjow's men, although many lackeys of the World Government had already fled across the borders into the neighboring countries.

After his triumph, Artur organized a huge rally in Minsk and announced the political goals of the new government. Other major events followed in all bigger cities across the country.

Now it was time to act and to secure the won power by all available means. One important tool to influence the masses in the sense of the revolution were the media, that were repeating Tschistokjow's principles again and again.

In return, many journalists and editors of the past, who were viewed as traitors of the people, fell victim to a first execution campaign. At the end of February, the Rus finally expanded the revolution to Lithuania. Tens of thousands of people besieged the headquarter of the Lithuanian government in Vilnius and forced the local administrator to resign too. The Lithuanian police went over to the rebels and the small number of GCF soldiers left the Baltic country without resisting.

Artur made Mikhail Gromov, the commander of the Lithuanian section of his organization, to the interim prime minister of the tiny country. Soon after, the new rulers started a bloody crusade of revenge all over Belarus and in the southern Baltic.

Special units under the command of Peter Ulljewski showed no mercy on those who they regarded as collaborators and supporters of the World Government.

Tschistokjow did not talk much about these actions, but Frank and Alf knew that they were brutal and ruthless.

'We must destroy those who wanted to destroy the future of our children!' he just said.

Artur gave his men free rein to start their retaliation campaign, if they only followed his orders.

'We must be hard! There is no more room for mercy and forbearingness in this struggle for the survival of our nation, because our enemy is much too dangerous to fight him half-heartedly,' he was saying in these days.

However, sub-governor Medschenko, his closest advisers and some other members of the fallen regime, had already fled to Russia.

Furthermore, Artur expelled all the foreigners who had been brought to Belarus and Lithuania by the servants of the World Government. In this context there were still several riots in the bigger cities which were finally quelled by the police and Tschistokjow's troopers. Those, who did not leave the two countries voluntarily, were forced to go.

'It is done!' said Wilden, raising his glass while the villagers in the old church of Ivas cheered at him.

Frank had finally returned to his home village and enjoyed the short period of rest. Julia snuggled into his arm and Alf took another bottle of vodka from the table.

'My father will soon rent an apartment in Minsk,' said Julia.

'This will be necessary, he is our foreign minister now,' answered Frank and smiled at her.

'I hope we will find some peace now...,' answered the daughter of the village boss.

'Peace? This must be a joke. Now, the real troubles begin. Don't even think that the World Government will just watch our little revolution without doing anything,' remarked Alf.

'Let's forget all this crap for some hours, okay?' said Frank.

Without thinking twice he kissed Julia and the young woman winced. Then they kissed each other while Alf shook his head.

'What a nice end, isn't it?' he muttered and emptied his glass.

Frank and Julia did not pay attention to their grumpy friend. For a moment they banished all their sorrows from their minds. It was a wonderful evening.

Alexander Merow

Alexander Merow has been writing science fiction and fantasy novels since 2010. He has become well-known for his dystopian book series 'Prey World'.

Meanwhile, Merow has also finished his science fiction series 'The Aureanic Age' and his fantasy series 'The Antariksa Saga'. He is currently working on further science fiction and fantasy novels.

Merow is passionate about inventing detailed and lovingly crafted fantasy and science fiction worlds, something that has brought him a growing number of readers over the years.

Book Series 'Prey World'

Prey World I - Future in Chains
Prey World II - Children of the Sun
Prey World III - Hatred and Faith
Prey World IV - The Collectivists

'Prey World IV – The Collectivists'

After the revolution in 2036, Belarus and Lithuania recover under the reign of the Rus. But the attempt to expand the rebellion against the World Government towards Russia is accompanied by a lot of setbacks. Suddenly, a second revolutionary movement appears out of nothing and stops the advance of Artur Tschistokjow`s organization.

Soon, Russia is shaken by bloody conflict between the 'Freedom Movement of the Rus' and their new rivals, the Collectivists. Frank fights in the first rank once more as leader of Tschistokjow's trooper units. But this time it seems that he is already down on his luck...